"So, yeah, we made out," I heard myself announcing. Behind us the grandfather clock chimed twice. I wasn't tired at all, though I did wish we could go back upstairs to Kirstyn's room and go to bed. I already regretted breaking my vow of secrecy.

But how do you not tell your best friends you kissed your ex? Especially when you are so busy not telling them everything else, something has to be let out.

"I knew it," Kirstyn said, shaking her head. "Didn't I tell you she liked Luke?"

"You did," Gabrielle whispered.

"I don't," I insisted, thinking, *Wait, do I? No, no I don't. I can't. We're friends, just friends. Friends who kissed two days ago. That's all. I don't want more, I don't need more.* The last thing I needed was complications. "I totally don't."

Novels by Rachel Vail:

Lucky

Rachel Vail

HARPER TEEN
An Imprint of HarperCollins*Publishers*

HarperTeen is an imprint of HarperCollins Publishers.

Lucky

Copyright © 2008 by Rachel Vail

Library of Congress Cataloging-in-Publication Data
Vail, Rachel.
   Lucky / Rachel Vail. — 1st ed.
     p.   cm.
   Summary: As Phoebe and her clique of privileged girlfriends get
ready to graduate from eighth grade, a financial scandal threatens
her family's security—as well as Phoebe's social status—but ulti-
mately it teaches her the real meaning of friendship.
   ISBN 978-0-06-089045-2
   [1. Friendship—Fiction. 2. Popularity—Fiction. 3. Wealth—
Fiction. 4. Middle schools—Fiction. 5. Schools—Fiction.] I. Title.
PZ7.V1916Lu 2008   2007031700
[Fic]—dc22   CIP
                                          AC

Typography by Joel Tippie
09 10 11 12 13 CG/RRDH 10 9 8 7 6 5 4 3 2 1
❖
First paperback edition, 2009

1

OUR TOASTER IS MOODY.

When I got down to the kitchen this morning, just my sisters were there. I said good morning to them. Allison grunted. Quinn said, "Morning. Waffles?" She was putting three frozen waffles into the toaster, one for each of us.

"Yum," I said, but I couldn't wait, so I grabbed a Smoothie out of the fridge. "Where's my *Teen Vogue*?"

"Should be in the trash. How can you read that crap?" Allison said, grabbing the Smoothie out of my hand to read the label. "You like these?"

I shrugged. "I wake up hungry."

"I'd give anything for your metabolism," Allison grumbled, handing the Smoothie back to me.

"Trade you for your white sweater," I said between gulps.

"I wish." She kicked off her sneakers.

"You're both skinnier than I am, so shut up," Quinn

commented without looking up from whatever she was doing on her laptop.

"I'm not skinny," Allison said, yanking off her socks. "I'm *interesting looking*."

"Get over it," Quinn said. "Grandma didn't mean anything—"

"She meant *ugly*," Allison interrupted, stomping barefoot toward the back hall. "Whatever. Phoebe, did you take my new flip-flops?"

"No!" I yelled, trying to remember if I had.

The toaster lever popped up. "Phoebe!" Allison yelled at me from inside the back hall closet. "You're standing right there! Could you get the waffles? Come on. Quinn and I have to go or we'll miss our bus!"

"Oh, like the middle-school bus is so much later? Please!" I hate when Allison acts like she and Quinn are a team I'm too young to try out for. I am fourteen, not four, and she is closer to my age than Quinn's by three months.

I tossed my empty Smoothie bottle in the sink, and then, slowly enough to totally torture my sisters, opened the toaster door to check. All three waffles were soggy on the edges and hard in the middles, with little ice crystals still clinging to the tops.

"Still frozen." I closed the glass door of the stainless steel toaster oven and pressed the lever again.

Quinn's head jerked up. "Seriously? Retoasting?"

"No way," Allison yelled, coming back into the kitchen

with my new flip-flops dangling from her fingers. "You know the toaster gets insulted."

"No, only you do," I told her. "Those are my flip-flops."

"They're mine! You just stole them yesterday. Yours have the stripey thing, remember?"

"Oh, yeah," I said.

I found the *Teen Vogue* in my bag and brought it over to where Allison was standing at the sink, wet-paper-toweling invisible dirt specks off the edges of her/my flip-flops.

"Want to see the dress I found for my graduation party?" I asked her, flipping pages. "It's green. Do you think that's—"

Allison cursed and pointed at the toaster. Smoke was curling out of it. I cursed, too, and dashed across the kitchen. When I yanked the toaster door open, a huge ball of dark smoke exploded out.

The smoke alarm started blaring.

"It's not a fire," Allison yelled at the smoke alarm on the ceiling. "Just more exploding waffles." Dropping the flip-flops, she ran to open the sliding glass door to the deck and yelled back at me, "I told you, Phoebe!"

Quinn and I waved our arms in front of the smoke, guiding it toward the fresh air, until the alarm finally quit.

"Our appliances have scary amounts of personality," Quinn said.

"Like the thing," I said, laughing. "Remember? With Mom?"

3

My sisters both looked at me blankly.

"The electric tea kettle! Remember?" I unplugged the toaster from the wall and, holding out the cord like a sword, announced to my sisters, "Never be intimidated!"

They smiled then, too, at the memory of our mother's epic battle against our old electric tea kettle the last time she was on one of her occasional quitting-coffee kicks.

"Want to see a failure, girls?" Mom had asked that morning last fall, spinning around to face us.

All three of us nodded. Sure. We wanted to see anything she wanted to show us. When my mother is in the room it's almost impossible to look away from her.

She grabbed the electric tea kettle and thrust it out like a weapon, as water dripped guiltily from the spout. "A tea kettle's spout should stick out," she explained, her quiet voice controlled, intense. "But this one is snub-nosed. It's indented. You know why?"

We all asked why, trying not to smile too much as our cereal, forgotten, soggified in front of us.

"Why?" she repeated. "So that boiling water will spill all over the masochist who is making tea instead of going to Starbucks like a normal person!"

My father laughed.

"It's a design failure, Jed. Admit it—it drools!" She spun around toward him. "Look, it left a spot on my new silk shirt."

The spot was microscopic, if it existed at all. In her

4

sapphire-blue silk shirt under her black Armani suit, my mother looked, as always, flawless.

"You just have to pour it slowly, Claire," Daddy told her in his kindergarten-teacher voice. "Easy does it."

"That's so . . . tea-drinker," Mom answered, a small smile tipping up the corners of her mouth. "I'm not Zen enough for this malformed tea kettle? Fine, then, I'm not. Out it goes!" Mom slammed the full glass tea kettle into the garbage can. "That's it," she said, and turned to yank the plug out of the wall outlet so she could dump the base into the trash after the kettle. "Garbage."

Daddy smiled his crooked smile and murmured, "Oh, Claire."

"Let this be a lesson, girls," Mom told us, her chameleon eyes flashing deep sapphire. "We are the Avery women. Nobody—nothing—can intimidate us. We will never back down; we will never surrender. Especially not to moody inanimate objects!"

Daddy laughed again.

She pretended not to smile and continued. "We are warrior women! We are Valkyries! We will not—ever—allow ourselves to be bullied or mistreated! Right?"

"Right!" we answered her.

"You could have emptied the boiling water into the sink first, Brünnhilde," Dad said softly, wrapping his arms around her waist from behind.

She leaned back against his chest and, grinning up at

him, said, "Nah."

Then she turned to us, her smile broad and triumphant. "Go conquer the world, girls."

We scrambled out to catch our buses, grabbing bags and backpacks from our nanny, Gosia, on our way. We were halfway down the driveway before Allison asked, "What the heck's a Valkyrie?"

"No idea," Quinn said. "And why did Daddy call her Broom Handle?"

We all laughed the whole way to the bus stop. I was still standing there grinning after my sisters were long gone, when my best friend, Kirstyn Hightower, reached the corner and asked what I was grinning about.

I shrugged. "My mom was in rare form this morning. It was awesome."

"Mine was her usual lovely self—*do you really need that much cereal? Hundreds of calories!*" Kirstyn imitated. I rolled my eyes in solidarity. Kirstyn chewed on her pouty bottom lip. "You're so lucky, Phoebe."

She was right, I knew. I am lucky. Every time all that day when I thought of my mother throwing out the kettle, I had to smile and think of the word *Valkyries*, knowing what it really meant was me and my sisters and especially Mom.

So this morning, standing in front of the smoke-belching toaster, I announced to my sisters, "We're Valkyries!"

"Sure," Allison said, getting two Smoothies out of the

fridge. She handed the one she wasn't shaking to Quinn and said, "We're such Valkyries."

Quinn had looked it up, brainiac that she is. Apparently Valkyries are tough, beautiful girls who ride winged horses into battle in, like, Norse mythology. Or maybe it was in operas. Whatever. I didn't care; I was on a roll.

"Yes! We're Valkyries!" I said, doing my best Mom imitation. I picked the toaster up off the counter and held it high. It was heavier than I expected. A few crumbs fell onto my face and the floor in front of me.

"Take that, you moody inanimate object!" I yelled, and dumped the toaster right into the garbage can. "Ha! Conquered."

My mother strode into the room, the heels of her pumps clicking on the tile floor, and slammed her BlackBerry down on the counter.

"We are the Avery women!" I said, trying for, but I think not quite achieving, her level of complete confidence.

My mother pointed her long skinny finger at the toaster, which was bulging out of the top of the garbage can.

"What is this?"

"The toaster," I said. "It's . . ."

She yanked it out of the garbage. Coffee grounds, three Smoothie caps, and an orange peel rained off it onto the floor. "What the hell is wrong with you?" she asked me.

"It burned the waffles," I answered quietly. An orange seed fell onto her black pump.

"*You* burned the waffles," she said. "You don't throw away a toaster oven just because you set the heating level too high."

None of us answered. Nobody said, "No, it was on *light*," even though it was. Mom slammed the toaster onto the counter and wheeled around to face me.

"Do you know how much a new toaster oven costs?" Her eyes were the same steel gray as the suit she was wearing.

I didn't know what to say. How much? It had never come up before. My family never talks about money, never mentions how much things cost.

I shrugged, wishing Mom would crack a smile. I willed myself not to look at the small stain a bit of coffee ground had left on her bright white T-shirt.

"Guess," she demanded.

How much a toaster oven costs? Seriously? No idea. Thirty dollars? Three hundred? "I don't know," I said, eyes riveted to her bare knees. She never spills on herself.

She yanked open the glass door of the toaster oven and grabbed one of the charred waffles out. "This isn't even burnt. Grandma would just scrape off the black part. . . ." Mom grabbed a butter knife out of the drawer and scraped black into the sink, to uncover more black. The waffle had become coal. "There. It's fine. Eat it." She thrust it at me.

"No, thanks," I said, stepping back despite willing myself to stand still.

"Fine, I'll eat it." She bit into it and ash flew onto her white T-shirt, raining down in a flurry all around the coffee ground stain. She looked at her T-shirt, we all did, and the room was silent.

Cursing, she tossed the rest of the waffle into the garbage. "Spoiled brats," she said. "Throwing away a toaster oven like it's week-old roses." She grabbed her BlackBerry off the counter and stalked out, toward the stairs, muttering, "Who do they think they are, a bunch of princesses?"

"No," I whispered. The room was still reverberating. "Valkyries."

A look passed between Quinn and Allison, a look like they knew something I didn't. Neither of them grinned or laughed. After a few seconds, Quinn looked at me with terrible seriousness and said, "Guess not."

WALKING TO THE BUS STOP, past the new house still wrapped in Tyvek, I told myself to forget it. Sometimes people have their little psychotic moments and if you just move on, everything's fine again. Usually it's Allison who has the moments rather than my mother, but whatever.

I tipped my face up to the sun, grateful for the bright heat after weeks of cold drizzle, and decided to think about my party instead.

"Why are you smiling like that?" Kirstyn asked, coming up behind me.

"Just thinking—only five weeks till graduation."

"Did you write your speech?"

"I thought maybe you'd write it for me," I suggested.

"Right."

"I'll come up with something."

"You always do," she answered, tipping her head up, too. "I'm so over middle school it's not even funny."

"Tell me about it," I agreed, although, in truth, I was

having a great year. We all were.

"High school will be so much better," Kirstyn said.

"Absolutely," I agreed again. Whatever.

"Meanwhile," she said, "you can leave your graduation speech for the last minute, but there's so much we have to do like today on the party."

"I know it!" Oh, good, I thought. My favorite subject. "I'm so glad the five of us are doing it together."

"Oh, please, if I had to plan it with just my mother I would definitely shoot myself," Kirstyn said. "She's a wreck we haven't sent out the invitations yet. And this morning she said she won't take me dress shopping until I lose another five pounds."

I shook my head. "No way," I told her. "You're gorgeous! Don't lose any!"

"Well, you're lucky your mother is thin. It's my mother's own fault I have a big butt." She turned so I could have a full view.

"You so don't," I assured her. "No. Your butt is small and cute. Your mom is crazy—seriously, it's her own issue. It has nothing to do with you."

"You sure?"

"Positive," I said. "You're perfect. Hey, did you get the new *Teen Vogue*?"

"Yeah, I cut out some more pictures."

"Did you see the green Vera Wang with the wide-spaced straps?"

"Totally." Her eyes brightened. "As soon as I saw it, I

thought, this dress belongs to Phoebe."

"Really?" I couldn't help smiling.

"Oh, you totally have to get it."

"Thanks. Are you thinking of the peach one, with the thing?"

"The sash? Ew. I would totally look like a pumpkin!"

I laughed as Kirstyn pooched out her cheeks. She does have a sort of round face, but there's no way anybody'd mistake her for a pumpkin. The bus came squealing and groaning down the street and we climbed on, cracking ourselves up imagining how we would look at our graduation party wearing the most hideous dresses and looking like a human Thanksgiving centerpiece.

All through the morning Kirstyn and I drew pictures of ourselves in eggplant dresses and corncob dresses, and passed them back and forth. The only academic challenge we faced was not laughing out loud, especially once Gabrielle, Zhara, and Ann got in on it. Ann's drawing of herself trapped in a cauliflower outfit had us almost peeing in our pants. When the bell rang for lunch, we all hurried down to the cafeteria, slid into our usual lunch table, and opened our notebooks and our purple Sharpies. Party planning time. Yea!

"So, we really have to make our final invitation list," Kirstyn said.

"Who makes it . . . and dun dun dun duh . . . who doesn't," Ann said.

We laughed little, sort of polite giggles, at which point Ann started doodling all over her margins again. I tried to think of a way to help her out, but sometimes it's best to just let a lame comment die a quick death.

We all chewed for a few seconds, considering who should be included. I took a sip of my Sprite and said, "Maybe we should just invite everybody."

"Yeah, right." Kirstyn snorted.

"Seriously," I said. The middle school is so small, only about sixty kids per grade, sixth through eighth, that everybody gets to know everybody very well and there isn't really a popular group or anything. Everybody is friendly to everybody else, though of course you have the people you sit with most or have on speed dial. The five of us are tight, but we're friends with everybody. It's not like middle school in the movies, all catty and nasty. "It'll be fun, with everybody, and easier."

"The whole school?" Kirstyn asked, looking at me like I had announced I was actually planning to wear the eggplant dress she'd drawn.

"No!" I laughed. "Just the eighth graders."

"The other eighth graders will have their own parties to go to graduation night," Kirstyn said. "We wouldn't want to go to their parties; why would they want to come to ours? Like, if Bridget Burgess had a party, would you want to go?"

We all looked around at one another. The truth is, no,

none of us would want to go, and also there is almost zero possibility that Bridget Burgess would have a party anyway. "I guess not," I admitted.

Gabrielle laughed, tossing her hair back over her shoulder. "I guess *not!*" We all kind of laughed along. Gabrielle is gorgeous. She's always had the long tumbling dark hair and full, perfectly shaped lips; now that she's on the travel swim team all winter and the one star on our pathetic track team in the spring, she has the hardbody to match. High school boys drool over her. But we're her best friends. We know she's a total goofball.

"So?" Kirstyn uncapped her Sharpie. "Who makes the final cut, then? Should we write a list?"

"On the other hand," I said, "we are friendly with most of the people in the grade, so maybe it would be nasty to leave out just like eight or ten. I mean, it won't make that much of a difference, right?"

"Not that much, no," Zhara said softly. "An additional eight people would be about, um, six hundred dollars more, total."

We all kind of looked down. So awkward! Poor Zhara: Did she really think I was asking about how many *dollars* of difference it would make?

"Okay, what the heck, right?" I said, loud enough to break the awkwardness. "Let's just invite 'em all."

"Says the class president," Ann chimed in, her mouth half full of tuna.

"Shut up, Ann," Kirstyn said.

I shrugged at Kirstyn. "If some people don't want to come, they won't, and at least we're not being *exclusive*."

Every year in elementary school we got a talk from the school psychologist about how wrong it is to be exclusive, how hurtful it can be to leave somebody out. As if adults don't choose their friends? It's actually physically impossible to sit next to everybody at once. Please.

"True," Ann added. "We want to be *inclusive*."

"Sure," said Zhara, eyes glued to her page of budget calculations. "Phoebe's right, it doesn't make that big a difference, so we may as well, I guess. If everybody agrees."

"So, is it unanimous?" Ann asked. "We're inviting the whole grade?"

We all shrugged.

"Doesn't matter to me," Gabrielle said, crumpling up her lunch garbage and tossing it in a perfect arc into the garbage can.

"Fine," Kirstyn grumbled, recapping her Sharpie.

I smiled at her. We all always agree, ultimately. I was sure that within a few minutes, Kirstyn would forget she'd ever even had a different thought.

I was wrong.

"GETTING PSYCHED FOR THE party," a blushing girl named Melinda blurted, closing her locker, across the row from ours, at the end of the day. Her best friends, Jade and Syd, were blushing beside her. "I mean, you know, if I—I mean, if we—whatever. I mean, it's gonna be so awesome . . . if we get—"

"Great!" I interrupted, smiling at her.

"Okay, bye!" Melinda barely managed. They all dashed away, latched to one another's arms, whispering about how embarrassing that was.

I shrugged and turned back to my locker. As I gathered up my stuff, I asked Kirstyn, "So, what else do we need to figure out? Anything?"

"We'll have to order more invitations, for one," Kirstyn said sharply, slamming her locker shut. "My mother's going to freak."

"You guys," I said to the other three. "Wait until you

see these invites Kirstyn found. They are so cute."

"I can't wait," Zhara said.

"I guess I'll call the place when I get home and up the order by a dozen." Kirstyn grimaced, then swiveled her icy stare toward Ann. "Ann, did you ever call the Crazy Balloon Lady from Pleasantville?"

Ann slapped her hand over her mouth. "I'll call tonight," she said.

Kirstyn slid her eyes away.

"Sorry," Ann mumbled. "I'll write myself a note." She looked nervously from me to Zhara to Gabrielle. Kirstyn had been freezing her out all day. Ann was looking increasingly wrecked.

"Well, see you guys later," Zhara said quietly. She's the only one of us who doesn't do track, so she headed toward the early bus.

"Bye," I yelled after her. "Call you later!"

We all gathered up our book bags and our clutches, and hurried down to track practice. As we changed into our uniforms, Kirstyn bent close to me and whispered, "Ann's all like, we should include everybody, but the thing is, I am seriously not supposed to say this to anybody, but my mom is a little concerned about Ann's family."

"What about them?" Actually, I'd been the one who was all like everybody should be included, but that was obviously not the point.

Kirstyn twirled a wisp of her soft blond hair above her

17

forehead. "My mother wouldn't go into details," she whispered. "But, you know, Ann's family isn't exactly, you know, quite as comfortable, so . . ."

"You think they . . ." I was whispering, too. "You think Ann's family can't *afford* the party?"

Kirstyn shrugged.

"Wow." I'd never really thought about that possibility before. "Seriously?"

"Ann's mom called my mom and was all like, do we have to hire a photographer? Couldn't we just buy some of those crappy disposable cameras and let the kids take pictures of themselves?"

"Really?"

"I know, hideous. But I was eavesdropping on the phone upstairs so I heard her. Of course my mom was like, *Well, that might be a thought. . . .*"

We headed toward the sinks to check our ponytails. "Also," Kirstyn whispered, "you know how everybody was supposed to give me a check for the down payment for the club? Ann didn't."

"Why not?"

Kirstyn just raised her eyebrows.

"Did she say anything?"

"No," Kirstyn admitted.

"Maybe she just forgot," I said.

Kirstyn closed her eyes slowly. "Maybe we should just forget the whole thing."

"What do you mean?" I kind of shrieked. "Forget the party?!"

"Phoebe, *shh*! I just mean, maybe we're making too big a deal of it."

"Of what?" I grabbed her and pulled her into our locker row.

"Graduating," Kirstyn whispered. "Maybe we should just say, *Hallelujah, we're out of here,* and move the heck on."

"Come on, Kirstyn," I said, cramming my stuff into my locker. "It's going to be the best party ever! It's, what did your mom say? It'll be a night we'll all remember the rest of our lives."

"My mother. She's even more excited for this party than you are. She's like in heaven, planning it." She blinked her big blue eyes at me. "It's destined to be lame, Phoebe. No older boys will come to a middle school graduation party."

"Oh," I said, finally understanding.

"I'm not just thinking about Justin Sachs, Phoebe. I don't even like him anymore and you know it. It's just, face it. We're inviting all the same loser dweebs we've known since they were wetting their overalls in pre-K. What's the point?"

"The point is us."

She shrugged. "Things don't always just work out, you know."

"Sure they do," I said.

She shook her head. "You have no idea, Phoebe, you really don't."

"Seriously, I swear. With your mom planning it? And the five of us?" I gave her my most confident smile. "This party has to be great. Screw Justin Sachs. But you gotta give Ann a break, huh? You've been crazy harsh on her. You know it. She's just a little spacey, lately. So what? Ease up, okay? Let's go."

I started out toward the track, but Kirstyn didn't follow. When I turned around, her eyes were blazing at me.

"She's not the only one who didn't pay."

"Who else?"

"You."

"I paid," I said, smiling. My face was heating up, but that was ridiculous; I remembered getting the check from my mother like two weeks earlier. "My mom gave . . ."

She grabbed her notebook out of her locker, opened to a middle page, and thrust it toward me. I looked down at her neat chart, with her cute rounded letters and ruler-straight lines drawn in purple. The only two without Xs in the down payment boxes were ANN and PHOEBE.

"I didn't pay?" I dug my clutch out of my locker and unzipped it. "Are you sure?" I asked, pulling stuff out of it, kneeling on the cold painted locker-room floor. "I'm pretty sure I got the check from my mother—Yes, I remember giving you the check! We were over by the . . ." But then, beneath old notes, pens, gum, my cell phone, and two tubes of MAC lip gloss, I found the crumpled check my mother had written. "Oops." I handed the check to

20

Kirstyn. "Sorry about that."

She held the crumpled check pinched between her pointer and thumb tips. "No problem. Hey, so can you sleep over Friday or not?"

"Oh, yeah. Of course." Whoops. She had asked me on Monday. I'd forgotten to ask my parents but I knew they'd say yes; they always did. All five of us love our sleepover parties; we talk ourselves hoarse and by dawn we can't stop laughing. Allison thinks we act like second graders but we don't care; we love ourselves.

"Good," Kirstyn said icily.

"Sorry," I added. The more superior and tough Kirstyn acts, the more fragile I know she's feeling. Maybe her dad had been yelling more lately, or maybe she really was stressed about leaving our safe cocoon at Goldenbrook. Maybe she had tried to contact Justin, her ex, and he blew her off again. Ouch, that would make anybody prickly. Or maybe she really was fed up with middle school. Though I couldn't really see why. Everything was going great. But I smiled at her. "Okay?"

"Well," Kirstyn said, still standing there stiff, my crumpled check dangling from her hand. "Come by seven."

"All right. But Kirstyn, listen. Don't worry. Maybe Ann's check is in her clutch too," I said, willing her to put the check away and stop holding it like it was contagious. "I'm not the only space cadet."

"If she flakes out on the party and leaves us all in the

lurch," Kirstyn said, narrowing her eyes, "none of us will ever forgive her. Right?"

"She's not . . . nobody is flaking out, okay?" Yikes, you could see why half the girls in our grade were afraid of Kirstyn and the other half followed her around, begging for her attention. "It'll be the best party ever," I said, softer.

She wiped a fuzz off the check and slid it into an envelope stapled to the inside cover of her notebook. "It better be."

"Come on; we'll be late."

As we pushed through the heavy locker-room door, Luke Stoddard and his buddies walked by.

"Great day," Luke said.

"Absolutely," I answered. I watched him go, thinking, *Phew, that boy can sure wear a pair of soccer shorts.* Kirstyn was watching me watch him; I noticed when I pulled my eyes away. "What?"

"Don't even tell me."

"Shut up," I said, shoving her lightly on the shoulder. I'm trying to be better at that, at like, reaching out and touching people. Apparently I'm not so smooth at it yet.

She stumbled, then crinkled her tiny nose. "Hello, Phoebe? We're supposed to be moving forward, not back to sixth grade."

"I'm not . . ."

"Right. You just batted your flirty green eyes at Luke Stoddard. Can you say reruns?"

"I totally did not!" I protested, but my stomach was in a knot as we jogged up the hill toward the rest of our team.

Luckily, track was just as boring as always, and everything was back to normal at home after, too: Mom worked late, Gosia tracked down everything we couldn't find like mayonnaise (Allison) or a calculator (me), and Dad bopped around all goofy, helping everybody with homework while trying out a new song for his kindergartners about sharing—until we all screamed at him to shut up and stop sharing it with us.

School the next day was regular, too: four-minute bursts of everybody buzzing about the party—who'd get invited, what they'd wear, whether they should ask someone out to it—interrupted by deadly forty-two-minute stretches of teachers droning on about some academic thing everybody was too spring-fevered up to even pretend to learn. It was great. My cheeks hurt from smiling by fifth period.

Since Wednesday is our only nontrack day, Kirstyn and I rode the early bus home. That was fun, too, since we got into a whole theory about how global warming had melted everybody's brains slightly. I was just kidding, I thought, until I walked into my house.

"MOM!"

We stared at each other across the expanse of the kitchen. The first thing I noticed was that she was barefoot. Her perfect toes, just like Quinn's, lay in their rows like peas still snuggled in their pod. That's what I was thinking was weird at first, that Mom was barefoot in the middle of the day.

"Where are your shoes?" I asked her.

"My shoes?"

I noticed she was kind of squinting, and she was holding a bottle of medicine, and she was home. Honestly that's the order in which it occurred to me: barefoot, squinting, medicine, home.

"What are you doing?"

"I have a cramp," she said.

"Oh."

The thing is she never has a cramp. She never has anything wrong with her at all. She doesn't even wear glasses. She never had braces. Other moms are always getting headaches or going to the chiropractor or getting their boobs or their veins done, but my mother doesn't even stub her toe.

And she never comes home in the middle of the day. Once when I broke my arm, she came home before I went to bed, even though she had a work dinner she had to go to, so she had to head right back into the city again after she signed my cast. Seeing her barefoot in the kitchen when I walked in after school was as crazy as it would have been to walk into social studies third period and see her barefoot in front of the class.

"Is that why you're home?" I asked.

She rested the bottle and the cap on the counter and squinted up at me, like she was trying to see me more clearly, or figure out who I was.

"You have cramps?" It occurred to me that maybe I was the one in the wrong place.

"No," she said.

"Are you sick?" When she didn't answer right away, I felt the blood drain from my face. I have heard that expression before but never had the sensation, and it really does feel like that; you feel all the blood dripping down out of your skull and you can feel your brain, and your nose, suddenly chill.

"I just had to get out of the office and drive, and it

became clear to me what I had to do. Commit. It's a golden opportunity. Could you do me a favor?"

I ran around the center island to her side. Maybe there really was something wrong with her. Maybe she was seriously ill, and everybody knew it except me. How could my sisters not have told me? Ah, that brought the blood back up where it belonged.

I wanted to do the right thing, let her lean on me, or carry her up to her bed like she would have done for me. I realized I was almost as tall as she is, which meant I had grown again, or maybe it was just that her shoes were off.

I didn't know what to do. I lifted my hand to touch her arm, but that seemed too weird, stilted, awkward. Ack, she's Mom. She doesn't need help, ever. I tried to pretend I was Quinn, who would know how to act.

Meanwhile my hand hovered in the air, as if I were waiting to be called on by a teacher. By the time I realized that, it was too late to drop it without being really conspicuous, so I just let it hover there, as if that's what I sometimes do when I am completely relaxed, just raise my hand, my gravity-averse left hand.

My mother looked at my hand with slight curiosity for a moment. I was about to explain that I was stretching, just stretching my arm, or checking the, um, air pressure, when she put the pill bottle in it and said, "Thanks, Phoebe."

It was the store brand of ibuprofen. That was sort of reassuring. She wouldn't be taking ibuprofen for some-

thing serious, I didn't think. Daddy gives me ibuprofen for a sore throat or an imaginary fever and sends me to school. It would be prescription stuff if something really bad were going on. Right? Or at least not the store brand.

"Can you get the cotton out?" Mom asked me.

"Sure," I said, poking my finger in and fishing out the long curl of cotton on top of the pills. "Why?"

Uh-oh. Maybe it was a trick question. Maybe I wasn't supposed to take it out, just answer whether I could? Maybe there was something disgusting about getting the cotton out? How long had she been standing there in the kitchen, girding herself to pull out the cotton? Was she about to spring into her shoes, dash out the door, and go back to work? Should I be doing something? What if she asked me to help her up to bed?

Oh, dread.

The picture of her leaning on me up the long front stairway was too frightening and melodramatic for me to imagine without going weak in the knees.

I recognized, as I was thinking all this, that I was kind of freaking out, and wondered if this is how it must feel to be Allison, who is constantly freaking out. Holding the bottle in one hand and the cotton snake in the other, I watched them both quiver.

"I just . . . can I have two?" Mom asked, closing her eyes. "Make it four. Four is okay. Damn derivatives market."

I dropped the cotton on the counter. I had never taken

pills out of a bottle, not even vitamins before. I poured out a handful of the small brown pills into my palm, chose four, and handed them to her. She tossed them into her mouth and swallowed.

"Do you want some water or something?" I asked belatedly.

"No," she said, squinting at me again, as if she was just realizing I was there. "Why are you home?"

"I—it's . . . Wednesday," I said, checking the clock on the microwave. "I don't have anything Wednesdays. Where's Agnes?"

"Agnes?"

"Our, you know, Agnes." Agnes! She was just always Agnes. It was sort of embarrassing to say "our." "The, our, you know, cleaning lady." Mom still looked blank, elsewhere. "She cleans Wednesdays, when Daddy does his after-school class and Gosia does the errands and then goes to pick up Quinn and Allison, and I take the early bus so usually when I get home Wednesday . . . Mom? Agnes."

"Agnes?" Mom blinked twice. "I had to let her go."

"Why?" I asked. "Where?"

Mom just smiled and exhaled. "Where indeed," she mumbled.

"Mom?" I wasn't sure even what to ask her, I had so many questions. "Why couldn't you get the cotton out?"

"Oh, it just gives me the . . . the heebie-jeebies," she said, shivering slightly. "Pulling the cotton out." She shiv-

28

ered again, picking up her BlackBerry.

"Really?" I asked her. "Why?"

She shrugged wearily. "Pulling it out of the little neck of the bottle . . ." She pressed a bunch of buttons on the BlackBerry and said, "No, come on."

Mom doesn't get freaked out by anything, I reminded myself. Not blood or the car throwing a rod or even, like, when the toilet in the powder room blew up.

"I didn't think anything . . ." I started.

"What?"

"Bothered you."

"Not much does." She tilted her head and stared steadily at me, her clear pale eyes unblinking. It made me feel clammy and apologetic. "Remember the last time the market tanked like this?"

"Um," I said.

"Son of a . . ." she said, clicking faster on her BlackBerry. "Five years ago. And I saw it coming, I knew it, felt it, I was totally shorted. I got a dot-picture on the front of the *Journal* later that week. Remember?"

I had no idea what she was talking about. Luckily she wasn't looking up, or pausing, so I didn't have to fake a response.

"That's when I went to Elysian—they all wanted me. But now here it goes, free-falling, two damn hours after I go out on a . . ." She stopped and looked up at me. "I'm having some trouble at work. Just between us."

I nodded. Normally when I am with my mother, at least one of my sisters, but usually both, are there.

"Oh, shoot, I better cancel those tickets. They better not have charged, please . . ." she said, dashing to the computer on the counter and typing furiously. "We won't be going to Paris this summer, to say the least."

"Were we going to Paris?" I asked. "After camp?"

"We're not. I gotta, ugh, sorry, hold on. Looks like Pfizer's moving, I have to . . ." She typed so fast and hard I thought her fingers might drill through the keys, through the granite counter, down into the cabinet below.

"No problem," I said. I should have signed up for chess class on Wednesdays, I decided, even though I hate and suck at chess. I hate and suck even worse at this.

"I don't want you to worry, it's just, I have to do a few things very fast, before Galen starts. . . ."

"Okay," I said, wondering when my sisters would get home. It's easier for me when she talks to them and I just listen or space out. My only memory of being a baby is of her holding me while she talked to other people, my sisters, my father, the phone.

"I have to figure out how to . . ." she said tightly, fingers flying, pounding. "See, on top of the very complex position I took with the fund, there's going to be a margin call coming in any minute, because I'm now under-collateralized on my own. . . . It's kind of complicated, if you want to know the truth, Phoebe."

I nodded again. Had I said at some point that I wanted to know the truth? I shrugged with one shoulder and checked the clock again. Any minute, they'd be home. Any minute.

"But I'm fixing it. And the fund, this is a golden opportunity. I had to go to the edge. I had to. Sometimes you just have to double down, that's how you change your luck."

"Uh-huh," I agreed. Sure, double down, go to the edge, whatever. A little trouble at work. If I wanted to know the truth. Uh, no thanks? We have to cancel a trip to Paris I didn't even know we were taking not because she wanted to go to Tuscany instead but because, it sure sounded like, we could not *afford* it. I didn't even know how to think about that. It didn't sound like a little trouble; my unshakable mother was kind of freaking out, right there in front of me, pounding at the computer like her fingers were nail guns.

I should never come home right after school, ever.

"The market can't keep going down," she mumbled. "Uh. See? It's up a quarter point already, Galen. That's good. That's . . ." Mom made another few clicks on the computer before she logged out. The screen flicked back to a picture of me, Allison, and Quinn smiling on top of the back bowls in Vail, holding our skis, from February vacation.

After she stared at it for a second or two, Mom straightened up, her posture suddenly upright, normal again. "Tough it out and we can make great things happen," she said. "Right?"

"Right," I said. "We're the Avery women."

Her head snapped toward me. She squinched her eyes, focusing intensely on me. She nodded as if I had just confirmed something. "Exactly," she said. Her phone started ringing. After glancing at it, she shoved it into her bag. Her BlackBerry buzzed. She grabbed it and opened her eyes wide. Her cell rang again inside her bag and her BlackBerry started ringing, too, in her hand. She cursed and then rushed toward the back door.

"Bye, Mom," I called after her, but she was already gone.

5

ALL ALONE IN THE SUDDENLY silent house, I wandered through the kitchen into the dark oval-shaped dining room (when's the last time I went in there?), trying to think about what had just happened with Mom but also trying not to. What I ended up thinking about, I guess as a compromise, was Kirstyn's poetry.

Kirstyn won the eighth-grade poetry contest in March with a poem called "Child in the Ghetto." It was really good, all about how this kid's family had practically nothing but pride, *no lamp, no table, but a floor so clean, to eat off it he was able* . . . It had really deserved to win. I was the first person Kirstyn showed it to, of course, and it almost made me cry, the pain and beauty in it. My poem was all about how peanut butter glues your mouth together. There was a mean little voice inside my head during the poetry ceremony saying, *How would Kirstyn know anything about a child in the ghetto?* Her life is just as comfortable as mine and I knew almost for a fact that she wrote the poem sitting on one of the new top-of-the-line leather recliners in their new media room downstairs. So it seemed sort of, well, cheating, to write about a child in the ghetto when the closest she's ever come to even knowing a child in a ghetto is listening to some rap music on her iPod.

But maybe that's where I would live soon.

Maybe I would be a child in the ghetto and have really, really clean floors. Because that would be all that was left for us to be proud of. I would hold my head up and make something of myself, if that's what happened, just like the child in Kirstyn's poem; I would dream of a better day.

Yikes, I thought. I'm not sure I've got it in me to be that noble. I like it when today is a good day.

Maybe I am totally overreacting, I told myself, and forced myself to smile. Of course, I thought, I am so blowing it completely out of proportion. Mom is not losing it, she's just in work-mode. I normally don't see her in the middle of the day, is all. It's nothing.

I tiptoed from the dining room into the gleaming front hall, where nobody but the pair of cherub statues on pedestals flanking the front door ever goes.

"Agnes?"

No answer. *She had to go,* Mom had said. No. *I had to let her go.* Well, she sure seemed gone. I wandered over to the living room, the family room, the sun room, the den— nobody around. I am fourteen years old and perfectly fine at home alone, that's not the point, it's just, honestly? I think this was the first time I ever was.

"Where is everybody?" I yelled. Nobody answered. I headed up the front staircase but stopped partway up and sat down. I wasn't sure where to go. I didn't want to go up, I didn't want to go down. Usually somebody was yelling at me to *Come downstairs!* Or, *Go to your room!* I might not always do it but then I knew at least where I was *supposed* to go.

I sat down, waiting, either for somebody to come tell me what to do or for an idea of my own, whichever came first. I leaned back against the wall and stretched my legs across the step.

If Mom told me something was wrong at work, she had definitely told Quinn and Allison, too. First. Right? Definitely. They're older. If I were her, I would have told them way before I'd tell me.

I dug my fingers into the navy carpeting that ran up the center of the steps as I listened to the grandfather clock tick in the living room and wondered when everybody would get home.

It's probably nothing, really, I told myself, and decided to think about whether we should have make-your-own-sundaes at the party or if that would be tacky and a mess. *Tick, tock, tick, tock.* Kirstyn wouldn't really want to get out of doing the party. She just wanted me to reassure her as always, which is fine. She's not as lucky as I am, her life

35

isn't smooth the way mine . . . Shouldn't they be home by now? Does Luke *like me*, like me? Should I wear my hair down for the party or half up or all up? What if I'm actually not overreacting, and we are seriously going to be poor all of a sudden?

What if something really bad is going on and everybody knows except me?

I was still sitting there on the middle step when Quinn and Allison came home with Gosia, laughing as they clumped up the back steps about something that happened outside school, and then going *shh, shh*—as if the worst thing ever would be me overhearing their secrets. Last year most of the time Allison and I were always together and Quinn got all serious, practicing piano like every free minute, her hair pulled back tight in a bun and her eyebrows practically crossing each other on her pale forehead. But now Quinn and Allison are always laughing together and I'm the one alone.

I hate that.

I hate Allison, I decided, still sitting there. She is such a wannabe. With her crazy new group of friends in their black nail polish and Sanskrit in Sharpie on their sneakers. Bleh!

Allison spotted me as she and Quinn crossed the landing above me. Hands on hips, she screwed up her face like I smelled bad.

"What?" I demanded.

"Why are you on the front stairs?" she asked me.

"I don't know," I admitted.

"Well, get up and tell Quinn I didn't cut school today."

"Allison didn't cut school today," I yelled to Quinn.

"Whatever," Quinn replied, going into her room and shutting the door.

"Shut up!" Allison growled at me, meanwhile. "You have the loudest voice in the universe! Do you want Gosia to hear?"

"Didn't Gosia just pick you up at school?" So it was Gosia they didn't want to hear, not me? Oh, hallelujah.

"Outside school, yeah. Are you coming up or not?"

"You cut?" I whispered, climbing the stairs toward Allison.

She grabbed me and pulled me into her room and, shutting the door behind us, said, "You have to help me choose a bikini."

"Because you cut school?"

"No."

"Oh," I said. "Okay."

Allison blew air through her lips. "I'm going over to Roxie's, along with, like, half the boys' varsity swim team, and I have to choose a bikini." She was talking as slow as Quinn talks normally, but making it sound like she had to because I was a mental defective.

"You look great in all your suits," I swore to her.

"Shut up!" Her hands went up into her thick wavy hair and started twirling.

"I totally mean it, Allison. I would tell you if you didn't, you know I would." I hadn't been in her room in a while. It was as neat as ever, and smelled good, too.

"True. You suck that way." She spun toward the full-length mirror inside one of her closet doors and groaned. For the past year or two Allison has been convinced she's fat and ugly and it's no use even bothering with makeup. She thinks her hair is impossible, just because it's thick, dark, and wavy. Her wide-spaced hazel eyes make her look like an alien, according to her, and her puckered mouth makes her look like a fish.

"You know who Tyler Moss is?" Allison turned decisively from the mirror.

"Um," I said. I hate quizzes. A picture popped into my head: broad-faced guy with rosy cheeks and short dark hair and light brown eyes who was in fencing with Quinn. "Tenth grade, swim team, fencer?"

"Yes!" Her smile grew huge. "He's seriously cute, don't you think?"

I nodded. "Seriously cute."

"I know it! Roxie said he asked if I was coming over."

"No way! He definitely likes you!"

She grinned even bigger and said, "We'll see."

"So, but, you and Roxie cut school?"

"Me? Cut school? Come on. Print or black?" She held up two suits.

I chose the one she was holding slightly higher. "Print."

"You think?"

"Try both and I'll tell you," I suggested.

"Okay," she said, her cheeks bright pink and eyes sparkling. "You have to get out, though, because if I end up having a bathing suit crisis, it is not going to be pretty. But Phoebe, wait right outside my door, in case I need you to look. And tell me honestly, brutally, what you think, right?"

"Absolutely." Right then I would have promised her anything. I headed toward the door. "Hey, Al?"

Allison was already back in her closet. "What?"

"What does *had to let her go* mean?"

She stepped out of her closet with both hands full of bathing suits on hangers. Allison is the only person I know who hangs up her bathing suits. "I hate every one of these. What does *what* mean?"

"Had to let her go," I repeated.

"Fired her," she said, dropping the suits on the bed. "Why? Who got fired?"

I wanted to tell her, as payment for letting me in, letting me be the one inside with Quinn out, but no. I couldn't, not without telling her the rest. Even though she had told *me* about Tyler Moss instead of Quinn. But still, I couldn't tell her about Mom.

"I read it in a book," I lied.

"Random. Okay. I said I would be right there and I need to have a complete nervous breakdown first, so . . ."

"Sure," I said. "Sorry."

"I wish I . . ." Allison started, then stopped, raising an eyebrow. "You okay?"

Mom was home. She can't pull the cotton out of medicine bottles. We might be poor. "All good!"

"Lucky you," she said.

I smiled, closing her door. In the hall, I sat down against the wallpaper, waiting for her to model swimsuits for me, hoarding the information about Mom, Mom's secret, in case it was a secret, in case she didn't want anybody to know except me, for some reason. *Just between you and me,* she had said. So how could I go right off and tell Allison, then, first chance I got? Mom trusted me.

I sat there congratulating myself about how great I was that I could keep a secret from my sisters when my whole life all I wanted was to be in on theirs, but I knew I wasn't really so great. The bigger reason I didn't tell Allison what had happened with Mom was because of how good it felt, for once, to be the one to know something first. It made me feel rich to have something my sisters didn't.

Also, I didn't fully get what Mom had said anyway.

And, if I said what I thought it meant out loud, it might be true.

6

I WAS EATING PASTA WITH BUTTER at the counter when Allison got back home from Roxie's house. Gosia, our nanny or housekeeper or whatever she is now that we are too old for a nanny, had a plate covered in tinfoil ready for Allison. Gosia is not just gorgeous but is also a master pasta-with-butter chef; nobody makes it as good as she does and it is our absolute favorite meal. For the first time ever, Allison said, No thanks, she had already eaten. She went straight to her room and closed the door, saying she had a lot of homework to do.

Gosia and I shrugged at each other.

"How did I turn out so normal?" I asked her.

"No idea," she agreed, and went back to the thick paperback she was reading. Quinn was in the living room, practicing piano. Daddy was in the den, listening to opera and paying bills. Mom of course was still at work. I called her and asked if I could sleep over at Kirstyn's Friday night. She said, Sure, sorry, gotta go. I put my plate in the sink and, with absolutely nothing else to do, went up to doodle on my homework.

Mom didn't come home while I was awake and Daddy went to a PTA meeting at his school. After I did as much stalling on homework as I could stand, I knocked on Allison's door. She said to go away and stop being such a little pain in the ass, so we were back to that, apparently. I went to my room and IMed pointlessly with everybody about the party and watched TV in my bed until I fell asleep.

I woke up the next morning to Allison screaming that she couldn't find the plunger for the wooden leg of her costume for her social studies project, she had put it right by her backpack and now where the hell was it? Gosia knocked on my open door as she passed it, holding a plunger. I checked the clock, cursed, and popped out of bed. I had to hurry or I'd miss my bus. As the front door slammed behind my sisters, I was yanking my jeans on. I grabbed my favorite T-shirt from the shelf in my closet. Gosia must've ironed it because it still smelled like the stuff she sprays on, which I love. I whipped my hair into a pony and, after a full two minutes with the electric toothbrush, swiped on lip gloss as I dashed down the stairs. As I slipped into my flip-flops, Gosia handed me my bag with all my stuff in it, including, I hoped, lunch, and an Odwalla Bar to eat on the way to the bus. "Bye," I said only to Gosia, since the rest of my family was long gone by then.

"Have a good day," she yelled after me. "Come back if you miss the bus."

"Are you kidding me?" I yelled to her, halfway down the driveway. A girl in Quinn's fifth-grade class used to get driven to school at least a couple times a week because other kids made fun of her on the bus. I think that family moved away. Toughen up, Allison said about her, and I totally agreed. We were all like, if you can't even handle the elementary school bus, how are you ever going to manage real life?

Kirstyn was talking practically before I got to the corner. While the bus wheezed its way down Beech Street toward us, I was trying to figure out what Kirstyn sounded like. I nodded when she looked at me. She smiled, relieved that I agreed with whatever it was she'd been saying. Just before we got to school I figured out what it was: It sounded like when somebody near me is wearing earbuds—noise and a beat but no tune, no recognizable words.

Luke was already in his seat, behind mine, when I got to homeroom. As I sat down, he jiggled my chair a little with his feet. Just barely managing not to fall on my butt, I turned around to shoot him a look. He smiled. I smiled back.

Ms. Alvarez, our homeroom teacher, mentioned that she was waiting, so I sat straight and smiled sweetly at her, my hands crossed in front of me on my desk. Ms. Alvarez sighed. She has a slight facial-hair issue but otherwise she is perfectly nice. She told us her announcements while I finished up the homework I hadn't had a chance to do the night before and then the bell rang. As I passed her desk, she said, "Phoebe? How's your commencement speech coming?"

"Great," I assured her. "Thanks!"

"I'd like a draft by Friday," she said.

"No problem." I smiled. "Bye!" I kind of drifted through the rest of the morning smiling, chatting in the halls between classes, nodding. *It's all good,* I must've said ten times or twenty.

I kept having this odd feeling like I wasn't myself anymore. Instead I was watching a movie about a slightly familiar-looking girl named Phoebe, and not just watching but really half watching, like a dull movie you kind of watch on a plane while you are also flipping through a lame issue of *People* magazine.

At lunch, after we made our way to our table past a few cliques of kids who casually mentioned they were looking forward to the party, wondered if there was anything they could do to help, and said how great one or the other of us looked that day, Ann announced that she had finally made an appointment with the Crazy Balloon Lady from Pleasantville. Kirstyn kept her eyes riveted to her notebook. Ann asked if anybody wanted to go to Pleasantville with her to look through the photo album of possibilities on Friday after track.

That woke me up.

"Friday?" I started to object: Since track ends at five thirty and Kirstyn wanted us over for the sleepover by seven, how would we have time to get all the way to Pleasantville and choose centerpieces? But Kirstyn stomped her flip-flop hard on my foot. I turned toward her. She was reading her notes in her notebook with intense seriousness, but then, very subtly, shook her head.

"After track," Ann repeated.

"Oh," I said. Kirstyn wasn't inviting her? How weird! "Um . . ."

"I'll come with you," Zhara said.

"Great," said Ann. "I'm just so indecisive."

"I'm not," Zhara said, taking a big bite of her sandwich. "I always know exactly what I like."

"That must be nice," Ann said, sighing.

I didn't get Kirstyn alone until after school, at track. Gabrielle is faster than we are, and Ann does shot put, down on the lower field (she mostly lies in the grass, looking at the sky; she has no interest in exercise of any kind but nobody gets cut from track and Ann's mother said she had to do a sport, to get her head, ironically, out of the clouds). Zhara hates sports and her parents think that's fine, so she was the only one of us not out in the sun, sweating her butt off four afternoons a week.

The boys on the soccer team were doing suicide sprints on the field next to us. We watched them as we jogged by. I think Luke flashed me a smile as he was turning around, but maybe he was just grimacing.

As Kirstyn and I rounded the far end of the track, away from Coach P, I got my chance. "What's the deal?" I asked her. "You didn't invite Ann or Zhara?"

"More running, less chatting, Pretty Girls," Coach P yelled. She always calls me and Kirstyn "Pretty Girls" and it is not a compliment. We don't care.

"It's not a party," Kirstyn whispered. "It's just a sleep-over and my mother is practically psychotic lately as it is, planning our party. Ann and Zhara would put her over the edge. You know how they are."

I shrugged. I thought they were pretty much the same as us. Apparently not. "What's wrong with them?"

Kirstyn gave me a shove like I was joking around.

Gabrielle passed us, lapping us, and slowed down a little when I grabbed the back of her shirt.

"Hi, speedy," I said.

"Hi, slowpoke," she said. Even though she's way prettier than me and Kirstyn, she's also a better runner; Coach P calls her "Bullet."

We all jogged together a few steps, before Kirstyn said, "Do you think we should get enough invitations to actually invite some of the tenth and eleventh graders, or just kind of, you know, let them crash?"

Gabrielle shrugged, speeding up. We sped up with her.

"Are we even sure we want them to?" I asked, trying to breathe deep and slow, like Coach P taught us. "I mean, there's something cool about it just being us, right?"

"Something pathetic," Kirstyn said.

"You think?" I sped up to stay in step with them. Was this a race all of a sudden?

"I'm so stupid," Kirstyn said. "I thought for a second you were serious."

I was being serious, but I had no breath to argue. I was concentrating on pumping my legs faster, faster.

"Hey, but seriously," Kirstyn said. "I say we go with the Sandra Pennington Photographers who always do such a nice job, and we'll each get a cute little album after. My mother already negotiated that with her. If we're doing this, let's do it right. Right?"

"Right," I said, because I had to, and because I couldn't say much more. I was sweating like a pig and totally out of breath as we rounded the corner past Coach P, who, for the first time ever, smiled at us.

"Whatever," Gabrielle said. "My mother says whatever everybody wants is fine, so let's do it up."

I glanced at her. She was barely sweating, her dark hair still neat in its perfect loose braid, her legs not pounding the track like mine but moving in smooth circles. She could have been pedaling a bike downhill.

"Exactly. And if some families can't pay for it," Kirstyn

47

continued, looking straight ahead, "or don't *want* to pay for it, fine. My mother says it doesn't matter, we shouldn't make anybody feel insecure or whatever. She's like, *we'll* pay the extra. We like to do it nicely, so, it's just not a big deal. She said she'll call your parents today and discuss it."

"Little albums?" Gabrielle asked dubiously.

"They're really cute," Kirstyn said, but checking Gabrielle's expression, rolled her eyes. "It's for our mothers anyway." She shrugged like she really couldn't care less.

I was totally out of breath. Keep running. Right, left, don't fall down. Don't think about if mine is one of the families who won't be able to afford . . .

"Phoebe's the one who'll look at it every day," Kirstyn said, shoving me into Gabrielle. I had to take a bunch of little steps to stay up and untangled. "Right?"

"Absolutely," I managed. "I'm just . . . getting . . . a cramp!"

They both slowed down with me, until we were walking. I raised one hand over my head and planted the other on my hip, to ease the stitch.

Kirstyn's face was red, but not sweaty. She gets so tense lately that Gabrielle will look down on her, think she's less than cool. "It's all good," I managed to say, trying to reassure her, but it didn't work. Her face turned even blotchier.

I attempted a smile but a wave of nausea rolled up my body. I put my hands on my knees and lowered my head.

"What's wrong?" Gabrielle asked. She sounded far away so I turned to look at her. Bad decision. Very bad. Black and bright swirled together in front of my eyes and I lost my balance.

I sank down onto the track. "Nothing," I was trying to say. "Everything is fine."

I rested my head on the cool red clay of the track to regain my balance. Above me I could hear them talking about me, and then Coach P asking what had happened.

"I'm good," I said. "Just . . . tried to . . . you know, keep up."

I didn't trust my legs yet so I just stayed there with my hot head on the cool ground, and my eyes closed.

"You okay?" I heard somebody else ask. Who? I knew that voice. No. He was way over on the far field with the boys.

I turned my head to the side. Cleats, covered in mud.

"What are you doing here, Luke?" Kirstyn asked.

"Just . . . just . . . I don't know. I thought she fainted."

I closed my eyes again but said, "I'm fine. Great. Just taking a short break."

Coach P yelled at Luke that he should get over to the boys' field and started yanking me up by the elbow. "Get up, pretty girl," she said. "Break's over."

I followed my elbow up. Luke was walking away, toward the far field. I could see his coach yelling at him. He raked his fingers through his wavy brown hair and shook the sweat off his hand without looking back. His last name, Stoddard, stretched across the shoulders of his soccer shirt, and one of his socks was sagging a bit below his calf.

Coach P gave me a little shove. "Make a runner of you yet, Miss Class President," she sneered. I turned to roll my eyes at Kirstyn, who grimaced.

When Coach P blew her whistle right in our faces and yelled for us to hit the locker room, Kirstyn and Gabrielle turned and started heading there. "Wait up," I called, jogging to fall into step beside them.

7

"YOU OKAY?" GABRIELLE ASKED as we opened our lockers.

"Yeah, sure. Just not as fast as you guys, I guess."

"What happened?" Ann asked, already sitting on the bench, ready to leave.

"Nothing," I said. "Just took a short break. On the track. On my face."

Kirstyn made sort of a *humphing* sound. I hunched down a little so I wouldn't feel quite so hulking, standing there over her. "Did I grow again?" I asked. "How tall am I planning to be? This growth spurt is turning into a marathon, seriously."

Kirstyn flipped her hair over her head to fix her ponytail. "If you're interested in Luke, you should say so." She flipped back up and rested her hands on her hips. Usually when I ask about if I am growing grotesquely tall, she reassures me that I look great.

Ann's eyes darted between me and Kirstyn. Gabrielle,

meanwhile, buried her head so deep in her locker she looked likely to get swallowed up by it.

"I'm *not* interested in Luke," I told Kirstyn. "You're the one who keeps talking about him, not me. Maybe *you* like him." I put my hands on my hips, too. Enough, already.

"Ew, as if," she said. "I get paid for babysitting, thank you."

"Yeah, right," Gabrielle said, emerging from the locker with her long hair loosened from the braid. "As if you ever babysit."

"Well if I did, I'd get paid."

They both started cracking up. Ann stared at her feet. She babysits.

"But seriously, Phoebe," Kirstyn said, pulling a fresh T-shirt on. "If you're honestly not into him, you are leading him on. You need to tell him, *Yo, I broke up with you two years ago, it's over. Move on.* He's like a lovesick pup, following you around. It's kind of sad, don't you think?"

"Aw," said Gabrielle. "A puppy, yeah, with those big sad eyes of his."

Luke is so not the lovesick pup; if anybody was that, it would be Kirstyn, the way she constantly monitored whether Justin Sachs was online or not. But obviously I couldn't say any of that to her. She has it harder than I do, I reminded myself, and as cute and fabulous as she seems, I know she gets jealous of me and my life sometimes, and it makes her act mean. She is right, I am a lucky person;

everything comes easy to me. I can afford to be generous with her.

"It's not, it has nothing to do with that," I said instead. "Anyway, whoa, I practically belly flopped onto the track there, huh?"

But Kirstyn wasn't letting it go. She turned to Ann and explained, "She looked over at Luke and just swooned." Kirstyn smiled at me, but it was a cold smile, no happy humor anywhere in it.

"We went out for like five minutes, forever ago," I said, trying to keep it light. "Who even cares?" I shrugged at Gabrielle and Ann, who both shrugged back.

"Not me," said Gabrielle, slamming her locker shut.

"Me neither," Kirstyn said. "And I know Ann doesn't care."

Ann opened her mouth and let it hang there.

"Exactly," Kirstyn said. "So that leaves . . ." Her head tilted toward me.

I admit, I was getting pissed off. I reached back beyond Justin Sachs to sixth grade, where she was accusing me of getting lost. "Me and Luke are such ancient history nobody remembers it but you, Kirstyn. I mean, you don't like William, right?"

"William!" Her cheeks reddened immediately, as I had known they would.

"Yeah, William," I said. "We're friends now, me and Luke, just like you and William, just like . . ."

"William and I are not exactly friends. He's so imma-ture. . . ."

"Well, so is Luke." I yanked off my own uniform. Okay, Luke is actually not immature, but we're friends and that's all. What's past is past. I don't like him, I don't, because why would I? We went out in sixth grade, back when Kirstyn was going out with William and the four of us were like the center of the center and we were all practically babies.

I mean, it was good then, sweet, even when Luke got that weird haircut that made his head look like a rectangle; so much better than seventh grade, trying to get the eighth graders to notice us past Gabrielle. Actually, seventh grade was really fine, too, but back in sixth grade, Kirstyn and I and William and Luke rode bikes together after school, hung out by the swings at lunch, swam in my pool almost every day in June.

Well, anyway, that was a long time ago.

"You girls finished torturing each other yet?" Gabrielle asked.

"Almost," Kirstyn said, and the three of them laughed. I didn't. We finished getting ready without talking, and headed outside.

Okay, maybe I have been kind of more, well, aware of Luke lately. But even if Luke is distractingly cute this spring, with his hair hanging down, curling on the ends by his ears, it doesn't matter. I've known him way too long for anything else to evolve between us. He's a nice guy, is all, and there's no reason we can't be friends. I don't like him and he doesn't like me. That's how it's been for almost two years, I told myself, and how it will always be.

It is interesting, though, that the more people talk about a thing that is absolutely not true, the more it can start to feel a little bit true.

Kirstyn's mother picked us up in the circle. She asked if Gabrielle and Ann wanted rides but they said no, they were all set. Kirstyn settled in, shotgun, and flipped down the mirror to check her teeth. She does it all the time lately; she says she lives in dread of having a poppy seed stuck in her teeth and not knowing it. I would've told her there was nothing there, if she'd asked me. I took the seat behind her mother. I wasn't sure if we were in a fight or what. Luckily Kirstyn's mother talked nonstop so we didn't have to.

She was going on and on about the party, something about how using the white tablecloths the club had standard would be fine, but maybe alternating pink and red, or doing overlays (whatever that is), would be so much cuter and why not? I looked out my window and Kirstyn looked out hers. I didn't want to think about the tension between us. I decided to think instead about what it meant that Luke had run over when I was facedown on the track.

We turned onto Willow Road, past the Magnolia Estates sign with its neat bed of all white flowers growing evenly beneath it, contrasting cleanly with the deep green of the surrounding grass. Nothing messy could happen here, Daddy said when we drove past it, coming home from the airport after spring break last year. No, Mom had said, the Committee wouldn't allow mess. They both snickered. They thought we were all asleep in the back, but I was faking.

Kirstyn's mom, who had apparently run out of stuff to say about the party she was planning, oh, wait, *our* party, started in on the neighbors. "Looks like these new people are using Lansdowne Landscapers." We passed the first house, and she cocked her head at the pair of trucks in the driveway, then rubbed her finger against her thumb, her sign for a lot of money. "But they're the best. Those other guys, what's-it-called—so crappy looking. They barely trim the hedges. But I guess if you want to save your pennies, you get less service and it shows. Anyway, that's good, Lansdowne. Maybe they'll put in some trees or something for those poor people, all exposed to the street like that." She clucked her tongue pityingly and looked at me in her rearview mirror. "These bald lots are so tacky, don't you think?"

I shrugged again. I don't really have many opinions about landscaping. Kirstyn's family was one of the first to move into Magnolia Estates, so their trees and hedges are the highest. Ours are way higher than the new people's at the front end of the street, but not as high as Kirstyn's family's. We moved to our house four years ago. But really, what do I care about the height of hedges?

"So nouveau," Kirstyn's mom continued. "Especially with all our houses now practically cheek by jowl, you know what I mean?"

I had absolutely no idea what she meant, so I said, *"Hmm."* Didn't even slow her down.

"Oh, look! They got the garage addition, like your family did. Smart," Kirstyn's mother added as we passed the new house diagonal from my own. "We only have the two-car. Ridiculous, really. They're coming from California, three boys," she said flirtatiously. Neither Kirstyn nor I said anything. "And I heard they're putting in a squash court."

"Yeah?" I could care less about a squash court. She had slowed the car to a crawl. Just please go up my driveway, I silently begged, or let me out here.

"I love when new people move in," Kirstyn's mother said.

She and Kirstyn had come over the first day after we moved in; Kirstyn was carrying a plate of cookies and her mother had what my father described as a *very* nice bottle of champagne. Before that, Kirstyn had barely noticed me—back when I lived on McNealy Street and she was the princess of third grade.

"Can you believe the Greens?" Kirstyn's mom asked. She had practically stopped the car.

I had no choice. "What?" I asked. Roxie Green,

57

Allison's new best friend, had moved here last summer, into the house Kirstyn's mom was pointing at, across the street from ours.

"You know they bought this house, next door to their first one. I was their broker." She made her finger sign for *mucho dinero* again. "Did you know they turned this one into a giant recreation center?"

"Yeah," I said vaguely.

Kirstyn hadn't budged or said a word. I decided not to look at her, let her cool down. Everything would be fine later, it always is. What was she even so mad about, anyway? Luke?

What if Luke actually likes me, likes me?

"So fabulous," her mother continued. "Indoor pool, full-court basketball, a yoga studio and giant steam room upstairs. All designed by you-know-who . . ."

I looked where she was pointing, at the huge house wrapped in Tyvek, with two giant green Dumpsters in the driveway and lots of machinery in the yard. "Cool," I said. "I should get home."

"Sorry!" she said, and whipped the minivan like it was a sports car into a right-angle turn, and zoomed up my driveway. "Ask your mom to call me," Kirstyn's mom said. "I've left her a few messages but I guess she's so busy. I don't know how she does it, working full-time with three active daughters, but I guess she has a lot of help. . . . Anyway, I want to talk to her about the party, ask her what she thinks about overlays. . . ."

I willed Kirstyn to look at me, smile her meek apologetic smile she uses after she's been bitchy to me. Nothing. Great, the silent treatment, one step worse on the Kirstyn emote-o-meter than biting sarcasm, just up from full-out tantrum. She might as well have been a statue in the front seat. Fine, I thought. Whatever, I could wait. I'm just lucky to be so uncomplicated. There's nothing to figure out with me—what you see is what you get. Life is good and I bump along with it. Maybe it's better to be deep and poetic and moody, like Kirstyn or even Allison, but honestly, I was thinking, I'm happy to be happy.

Halfway up the driveway Kirstyn's mom slowed the minivan down abruptly. We all bucked forward. My mother's Porsche was in front of the house, and my father's Jeep, too—neither of them in the garage—and also a cream-colored Jaguar two-seater.

"We weren't invited to the party?" Kirstyn's mom asked laughingly.

I sat there staring at the cars for a few seconds, trying to figure out what it meant. I couldn't. It made no sense. Something must have happened. What? I jumped out of the car and slammed the door shut behind me, running as fast as I could up the driveway and through the gate and up the walk into my house, where I was hit with an intense blast of cold.

"What's going on?" I yelled, slamming myself through the mudroom door.

8

"*Shh*." Gosia was on me in a second, taking my bag and pulling me into the kitchen. "You want a snack?" she whispered, fake-cheery.

"No," I said out loud. "Why are they home? And who's here?"

"*Shh*," Gosia whispered again. "Sit down. Have a snack."

"Stop it, Gosia, seriously. What's going on?"

"Phoebe," I heard Allison hiss from the back stairs.

I ran toward her, kicking off my flip-flops.

"Shut up," Allison said, turning around. She took the stairs two at a time. I raced behind her. Instead of turning left to the upstairs den we have to cross to get to our bedrooms, she went right into the guest wing, where we almost never go unless my cousins from Oregon are visiting, and even then not so much. It smelled different in the hallway there, like Pledge, and the carpet was brown, thick and soft like moss, so my feet sort of sank into it.

We passed the wall of school pictures of Quinn, Allison, and me—every school picture and class picture of each of us from nursery school on up, hung in identical Pottery Barn black frames with white borders, put together by Gosia. I couldn't help noticing as I passed that Quinn, who is cool now, was seriously dorky in the early years of elementary school. Who cut her bangs? They were like tacky, badly hung window valances.

I followed Allison into the second guest room. She kneeled on the floor right next to Quinn, who was perched on the edge of the bed. They both hunched toward the night table, heads bent close together.

"What are you guys doing?" I asked.

"Shut up!" Allison whispered fiercely. "What's wrong with you?"

"*Shh*," Quinn breathed without lifting her eyes.

I knelt down beside Allison and saw they were bending their heads over an old baby monitor that was crackling with static. I listened, too, but could barely make out the voices under all the annoying static rumble. I wanted to ask what they'd heard so far, and also how they had managed to put the other end of the monitor wherever it was Mom and Daddy and the stranger were, not to mention where they even found those old things in the first place, but I knew better than to say another word.

"How it all shakes out," I heard somebody say, a man,

so either Daddy or if the stranger was a man, him. Quinn and Allison made eye contact with each other but not with me. I cannot stand being left out. It's so incredibly unfair of them. I'm not a baby, no matter how they act sometimes. Hello, who was in your room yesterday helping you choose the print bikini?

"What?" I whispered. I wanted it to sound fierce and not whiny. I didn't completely succeed. Allison glared at me. I clamped my jaw tight to keep from saying more or worse, and rubbed my freezing arms.

We heard a door shutting and some loud footsteps, which meant probably they were in the foyer, because the floor there is marble and it echoes.

Quinn switched off the monitor. "We don't know, exactly."

"What DO you know?" I demanded.

"Shut up, shut up, shut up," Allison whispered through her clenched teeth. She tightened her grip on her tennis racquet and lifted it slightly off the floor. If Quinn hadn't been there she might've smashed me with it.

We heard footsteps again, closer this time but less loud. They must have been heading toward us, maybe to the back door, which is the one adult guests are usually shown to, near the bottom of the back stairs.

"Let's go," Quinn said, shoving the monitor into the cabinet of the dresser.

Quinn and I followed Allison down the hall, out of the

guest wing—Quinn closed the door to it quietly behind me—through the upstairs den to the upstairs landing, and down the hallway to our rooms. We passed mine on the right and Quinn's on the left to go to Allison's, just beyond Quinn's, before Mom and Daddy's. Quinn closed Allison's door behind us. I climbed up onto Allison's high brass bed and grabbed one of her million pillows to squish, reminding myself that the more I shut up, the more I would hear from my sisters about what they knew.

They kept looking at each other like they weren't sure they could trust me. I swear I was stopping myself from having a total tantrum only by using all of my willpower—and maybe also mangling the little pillow helped.

Finally I couldn't take it anymore and I blurted out, "Is somebody going to tell me what's going on or do I have to go down there and ask *them*?"

Allison threw her racquet onto her sofa. "I told you she'd react like this, didn't I?"

"Allison, chill," Quinn said. She sat down on Allison's bed across from me and leaned against the footboard. I guess it was uncomfortable because she held out her arms for a pillow. I yanked one of the huge ones from the back and tossed it to her. There was practically steam shooting off the top of Allison's head; she hates when people mess up her bed. But I could tell she was trying to be cool, not let Quinn think I could control my temper better than she could. Which I totally can. Allison grabbed her racquet again and paced between her bed and her sofa.

Quinn sighed. "The thing is, we don't really know any-thing," she whispered.

"Tell me what you think."

"You can't say anything to Mom or Daddy," Quinn warned.

"Obviously," I said, leaning forward.

"We're totally serious, Phoebe," Allison growled at me. "No hinting, no asking, nothing."

"Would you give me a break for one single second?"

"Okay," Quinn said. She was mashing a small white silk pillow between her hands. Quinn, who is always in control, who is so cool and calm my father calls her Zen sometimes, looked seriously tense, and that, more than anything else, was making my stomach clench.

"We're not sure," Quinn said. "But it sounds like . . ."

The door opened, and my parents stood there, pale, looking at us.

"Hey," Dad said.

"Hi," we all answered. He was holding Mom's hand. With her other hand she played with the little sapphire she always wears on a chain around her neck.

Dad cleared his throat. "Sorority meeting?"

I made myself smile. Quinn and Allison faked just as unconvincingly.

"So, um, Mom and I . . ."

We all waited. If this were a movie, I thought, he'd tell

us they were splitting up, after an opening like that. But he didn't continue. We all just sat there waiting.

He let out his breath and started over. "We're going out for a drive." Mom turned to him, evidently surprised at this news. "Okay? We're going for a drive."

"Okay," Quinn said.

Mom let go of her little sapphire and nodded slightly.

"Okay," he said. "Quinn, your SAT tutor is downstairs, and the tennis guy . . . is . . . he . . . he . . . can't come . . . today. Okay?"

"We don't care," Allison said. "Our court has a puddle on it, and . . . and we hate tennis lessons anyway. Right?"

I nodded. I actually do hate tennis. But Allison loves it. I couldn't look at her so I kept my eyes on my fingernails.

"So," Dad said, smiling fakely. "Oh, and just tell Oliver when he comes for your piano lessons that, ah, we'll give him a check next week. Okay?"

Quinn and I nodded.

"Okay," he said again, facing Mom. "We're going for a drive." He pulled her by the hand and they left.

The three of us just sat there for maybe two minutes, until Quinn leaned forward and said, "I think some people Mom works with have screwed her over."

"Really?" I asked. "Her friends?"

Quinn nodded. "Well, she thought they were friends. You never know."

I shook my head slowly. Poor Mom.

"This is what I think happened," Quinn continued, tucking her hair behind her ear. "You know Mom invests huge money for people, right? Well, from what I can piece together, one of her big deals did really badly. Lost millions, maybe hundreds of millions of dollars this week. It's not just her—there's like six of them who decide together what stocks to pick, but—here's the screwed up part—the other people on her team all got together and made it seem like it was just Mom, like she went off on her own somehow and made this really bad call on a drug company. They're putting all the blame on her."

"I hate them," Allison said.

"Screw them," Quinn said.

"Yeah," I said, trying not to think about Mom in the kitchen twenty-six hours earlier, when she seemed as alone as a person could ever possibly be.

"So what's going to happen?" asked Allison. "Like, to us?"

"Don't know," Quinn whispered. "That guy who was here is her lawyer."

"She's not, like, gonna go to jail or something, right?" I tried to grin at my own stupidity but my sisters both stayed pale and serious.

"No. He's the, you know, other kind of lawyer, like not criminal," Quinn said slowly. "Business lawyer. It's bad, though. Seriously bad. They let Agnes go."

Allison's mouth dropped open and her eyes teared up.

"Agnes?" She sniffed and turned to look at me. "You knew! Yesterday."

I looked back and forth between Allison and Quinn.

"Did you hear Mom fire her?" Quinn asked me softly.

"I heard her say something," I answered, thinking fast, speaking slow. "I heard her say the phrase *had to let her go*."

Quinn nodded. Allison grabbed my hand. Quinn grabbed my other, then Allison's other. "This might suck." Quinn leaned in toward us, and we leaned in, too, so our foreheads were almost touching. "But we can handle it. We're the Avery women, right?"

"Valkyries," Allison whispered.

Quinn and I both nodded. "Valkyries."

Then my cell phone rang.

9

"HELLO?" MY HEART WAS POUNDING from how startled I was. My ringer must've been on superhigh.

"Hi this is Luke may I please speak with Phoebe?" Luke said practically as one word.

"This is Phoebe," I said. "Luke?"

"Yeah," he said.

"Hi."

My sisters were staring at me. I shrugged. Why was he calling me on the phone instead of texting me? Sometimes he texts *hey* and I text back *hey*. That doesn't feel weird. We sometimes even complain about our homework. Why was he calling me?

"Yeah, um, hey," he said.

Neither of us said anything for a while. It was odd. It seemed like he was waiting for me to explain why he had called me. My heart was still thumping. It was Kirstyn's fault, what she said about me liking Luke, making me all weird with him. Well, that and talking on my cell with him in front of my sisters, at a kind of awkward moment. Quinn whispered that she was going downstairs to her tutor.

I popped up and almost fell off the bed because I forgot to untangle my legs. Chill, Phoebe, chill.

"So, um," he said. "What's up?"

"Nothing," I lied. *Just found out my life is in the toilet, that's all.*

"You okay? You know, from, when you, like, fainted?"

"Fine," I said in a shockingly high voice. "Anyway . . ." The doorbell rang.

"Oliver's here," Allison whispered. "Hang up!"

"I gotta go."

"Okay," he said. "But, I mean, what are you doing?"

"Now?"

"No, next Tuesday."

"Oh, um . . ." What? I couldn't think. Next Tuesday?

"Just kidding," he said. "I meant now."

"Oh, just . . . um . . . nothing."

Allison glared at me impatiently. I turned my back to her.

"But, if, um," Luke was saying. "I mean, a couple of us were going down to the Shops, you know, to hang around, just, you know. How about you?"

"Me?"

He laughed. "No, somebody else."

"Obviously," I said. "Me. Um . . ."

Allison chucked her tennis racquet at me.

"Ow!"

"Well, anyway," Luke said, very fast. "We're gonna get some sodas, you know, me and William and I think maybe Dean. Maybe, whatever, get a slice at D'Amico's and, are you okay? Did you just say 'Ow'?"

"No," I said, rubbing my hip where the racquet had hit me. "A couple of us were thinking of going down to the Shops, too," I lied, walking out of Allison's room.

"Great," he said. "So maybe I'll see you there."

"Yeah," I said. "Maybe. Later."

Gosia was screaming up to us as I shut my phone and sped downstairs, one step behind Allison.

"You don't think he could be asking me out, do you?" I asked her.

"Have you made out with him at all?"

"No," I said.

"Then no."

"That's what I thought," I said. "Hey, how did it go with Tyler?"

She grabbed my arm and twisted until my knees buckled. "Never ask me that again."

"Okay. Sheesh."

"He is a jock, I am a nerd, and never the twain shall meet."

"Huh?"

"I said forget it!"

"Fine!" We never used to have secrets in my family.

70

I mostly let Oliver play during my piano lesson. Obviously Dad's musical genes missed me entirely. I knew Oliver wished he could just have Quinn the whole time; he has such a huge and obvious crush on her.

"Why don't you ever practice, Phoebe?" he asked, closing my level one piano book.

"Dunno," I said. "Sorry."

He bent over to pull some new Brahms music out of his bag for Quinn. "No sweat," he said. Cute butt, I thought. "I get paid either way."

That's what you think, I thought. "Oh, um, my dad said he'll give you a check next week."

"No problem," he said. "Hi, Quinn."

"Gosia!" I yelled, leaving them alone with the piano. "I need to go down to the Shops!" On my way into the kitchen I texted Kirstyn:

Shops? Pick u up?

She didn't text back right away so I texted:

U mad @ me?

Maybe I should've asked Zhara or Gabrielle or even Ann instead, I thought, and was about to try Gabrielle when Kirstyn texted:

I cd never b mad @ u!

Gosia came into the kitchen as I was texting Kirstyn

back that we'd pick her up in a minute. I dumped out my book bag, in search of my good sunglasses.

"Hey," Gosia complained.

"I'll clean it up when I get home," I said, on my way through the door. "Promise. We gotta hurry."

As she was backing out of the garage, Gosia turned on the music. It was new stuff, nothing I'd heard before. She stuck a piece of gum in her mouth and chewed to the beat.

"Can I have a piece?" I asked as I took one from her pack.

"Would it matter if I said no?"

"Oh, wait, we're picking up Kirstyn."

"Ugh," said Gosia, slowing down.

"Why don't you like Kirstyn?"

"Because she's a spoiled brat."

"She's just rich," I argued. "And pretty. All that is just stuff from her parents. You can't judge her on that."

"I don't," Gosia said. "I couldn't care less if she's on the cover of every magazine or has all the money in the world. Or none of it. She could say hello."

"She says hello!"

"Not to me," Gosia said, stopping the minivan at the bottom of Kirstyn's driveway. Kirstyn was there waiting in a cute new outfit, her dark Gucci sunglasses covering half her face. Gosia pressed the button to let the back door slide open and checked her makeup in the mirror.

Kirstyn jumped in and, taking one of the pilot seats in

back, said, "Hi, Phoebe!"

Gosia raised one eyebrow. She's the one who taught Allison. I slumped in my seat and said, "Hi."

When Gosia got the door closed and the car moving, Kirstyn leaned forward, as if there'd never been a moment of tension between us. "How was piano?"

"Brilliant," I said.

"He's so hot."

"Hot for Quinn," I said.

"Yum." She leaned back in her seat and looked out the window. "We should go by Fabio's and look at the shoes, even though we don't have dresses yet. Is that stupid? But I mean, we'll need metallic or beige anyway, right? You weren't thinking dyed-to-match, were you?"

"No."

"I know, totally tacky. That's what I was just telling my mother. Did you get cash or your mom's credit card?"

"Oh, damn," I said, and checked my wallet. One dollar. Eighty-seven cents in the change compartment. I asked Gosia as sweetly as I could, "Do you have any money on you?"

"Now you want my money?" Gosia asked.

"They'll pay you back," I said to Gosia. "Just take it from the envelope in the kitchen drawer. There's a couple hundred in it, right? I only want like forty."

"What are you going to buy for forty?" Kirstyn snorted.

"I'm not buying today, just looking," I said. "I mean in case we need a soda or a lip gloss or something."

"You pay me back," Gosia said to me, pulling into a parking spot. "Here's twenty. You get it from them and pay me back. I don't want to ask your parents for the money. Understand?"

I nodded. So she knew something was up. My heart pounded as I shoved her twenty in my back pocket and got out of the car.

"Don't worry about it—I have my mom's platinum card," Kirstyn said. "She felt bad after the tackiness of her dyed-to-match idea." She showed me her teeth.

"You're good," I told her, after seeing nothing was stuck in them.

Lowering the passenger-side window, Gosia said, "Call me when you want to be picked up."

"Okay." I was all shaky, my fingers icy despite the heat. What did Gosia know? "Thanks, Gosia." She pulled away after nodding gently at me.

I took a deep breath to steady my nerves.

"You okay?" Kirstyn asked as we started to wander down the strip of stores on the first stretch of the Shops, looking in windows at the card store, Mac's Pharmacy, Kimmel's Bagel Shop. "If you were anybody but Phoebe Avery, I'd think you were actually stressed!"

"Stressed?" I forced out a laugh. "No. You want to hear the funniest thing? My sisters rigged up our old baby monitor to spy on our parents!"

"That is fantastic!" she shrieked. "Don't even tell me you overheard them, you know . . ."

"No! Ew!"

"So what did you hear?"

"Static, mostly," I said, adding, when she frowned, "So far!"

We laughed together. "So far," she repeated. The sun was beating down hard and I thought about suggesting ice cream but decided against it. Kirstyn only orders the nonfat which pisses me off, and anyway I didn't really want to spend Gosia's twenty if I could avoid it. So we just wandered around talking about eavesdropping. "I have to try that," she said. "Baby monitor. I love it! Sorry I was a bitch today."

"You totally weren't," I assured her.

"My mom is just making me nuts," she whispered, grabbing my arm and pulling me close. "Three more pounds to lose or no dress. I'll have to wear that hideous organdy poof from my cousin's wedding last fall. Oldest flower girl in history. Just shoot me now."

"She won't make you wear that," I said as we passed the cell-phone store. "She hated it, too. She's just stressed," I told her. "You know how she gets planning parties. But even she can see you're totally gorgeous."

Kirstyn sighed. "I wish I could not care what she thinks. Maybe your mom could adopt me. I think I'd be sweeter if I lived in the perfect American family."

I tried to laugh but it kind of got stuck, and then Luke and William walked out the door of D'Amico's just as we approached it.

Luke said, "Hey," and William said, "What's up," and when we just nodded, William added, "Man, it's hot." I swear I could not even look at Luke at all. Thank goodness I had my sunglasses on.

After an awkward silence, Kirstyn faced Luke dead-on and said, "Funny meeting you here."

Please don't tell her, I silently begged him.

"Hilarious," he said, staring right back.

"Well, see you later," she said, and turned sharply away.

I started to follow her but turned back toward them. "Or, hey, it's still really hot out. You guys want to come over and swim?"

"Yeah," Luke said, his voice sort of squeaking. "Sounds great!"

"What about suits?" William asked.

"You can do shorts," I told him. "No big deal."

Kirstyn put her hand on her hip and looked at me, shaking her head slightly. "So much for shoes," she muttered.

"It's too hot," I said. "And I think Fabio's closes at five anyway."

I called Gosia and we all stood around waiting for her. I slid her twenty under her pack of gum when I got in the car.

"These guys are coming over to swim," I told her.

"I'm not," Kirstyn said. "You can just drop me at home, please."

"Why?" I asked, turning around.

She gave me a withering look.

"Youch," William said, the worst possible thing.

Kirstyn's eyes narrowed slightly before she slid them away and looked out the window. When we got to her driveway, she started to get out but Gosia drove up the hill. "Can you just open the door, please?" she demanded, her hand gripping the handle.

Gosia pushed the button and her door slid open. Kirstyn was out before it had moved a quarter of the distance.

"What's wrong with her?" William asked before Gosia had gotten the door closed again, so I just shrugged.

As we made our way around the circle at the top of her driveway, under the portico, I said, "She doesn't, um, enjoy, you know, swimming."

"She's a whack," William muttered.

Gosia tried to hide it but she was smirking; I saw it. Luckily she didn't say anything. Instead she turned on her music again and Luke leaned forward. "I love this album!"

"Isn't it great?" Gosia asked.

"Have you read the lyrics of that one about the train?"

Her eyes met his in the rearview. She nodded.

"I know it," I added lamely.

When we got to my house, I sent them straight out to the pool house around back and dashed inside to get my suit. "He's cute," Gosia whispered.

"Who?"

"Sure," she said, smirking. "Play innocent. Dinner's in an hour. Are he and William staying?"

"No," I whispered. "Just a quick swim. You really think he's cute?"

She nodded.

I tried not to squeal, *I know it!* Instead I asked, "Mom and Dad still out?"

She opened the door and the music answered me: I could hear Dad playing the piano in the living room.

"They okay?"

Gosia shrugged. She headed for the kitchen and I took the back stairs by threes, listening to Dad playing something I didn't recognize. I used to sit on the steps and listen while he played, even in our old house when we had an upright with a broken middle C. Mom bought him the grand piano for his forty-fifth birthday present. We had practically no furniture yet in most of the rooms in this house, because we had just moved in. He cried when the delivery guys started unloading it, and then Mom started crying, too. He only stopped hugging her when he went and sat down on the leather piano bench and started to play, tears still streaming down his cheeks at the sound of that huge thing. He played love songs and laughed at himself for being such a sap, but she shook her head and sat squished next to him on the bench, watching his fingers on the keys. He was still playing when I went to bed that night, Beethoven to Beatles and everything in between, so many songs I had never even heard him play before. It's the one thing still sure to uncrease my mother's forehead: sinking down into one of the couches we have now and listening to my father play.

I figured that's where she was. Part of me wanted to forget about the boys in the pool and just cuddle up with Mom on the couch. But I'm not a baby anymore. Also, right then Mom and I each had our own crap to deal with.

I ripped off my clothes and dropped them on the floor, put on my best suit, the green-and-white one Allison says looks hot on me, and flew down the stairs.

I ran from the back door across the yard in my bare feet to the pool, ripped open the gate, and, seeing the guys were already floating in the middle, dived into the deep end. The cold water hit my body from fingertips to toes like a shock-wave, and then it was quiet. I glided underwater to the shallow end to Luke's raft and flipped it. We ended up in a huge water fight, me, him, and William. When we were all panting, we each grabbed a raft and then floated around for a while, catching our breath, squinting at the sky.

"This is great," William said. "This is the life. Your babysitter's really hot."

"Shut up," Luke said.

"What? She is, right?"

"Yeah," Luke agreed. "I've had a crush on Gosia since sixth grade."

"You're both rude," I said, flipping over onto my stomach. I didn't need them comparing me to her. Also, I didn't think it was normal to mention sixth grade, when Kirstyn would've been in the pool with us. We would've been playing Marco Polo and nothing would've been weird.

I closed my eyes and floated for a while, letting the sun dry me off. Actually, this is nice, I was thinking. Old friends, hanging out together. There's something really great about old friends, how you don't even have to talk. You can just float and be perfectly comfortable. Well, almost perfectly. But maybe that's why there was a tiny part of me that wasn't in such a big rush to get this year over with—next year maybe everything would change.

Or maybe everything was already changing. Too fast.

"This is great," William murmured. "Hard to believe it's past six, and still bright as noon. It's like summer already. Hey, you know your party?"

"Yeah," I said.

"You think I could score an extra invite? There's this girl in all-county jazz band with me, and . . ."

"No problem," I lied. Though Kirstyn would swear on her life she didn't like William at all anymore, I knew she would freak out if he had a date at our party and she didn't. But what could I say?

"Awesome," William said, trailing his long fingers in the water. "My mom says no way we can get a pool, too much liability or something. You're so lucky."

I closed my eyes. Lucky. Yeah, except, maybe not so much anymore.

When I opened my eyes, William was on his back, his eyes with their long dark eyelashes shut and his hands behind his head, but Luke was lying on his stomach, staring at me.

"What?"

He didn't answer.

"What are these thingies for, these circles?" William asked.

I squinted over at him. His eyes still closed, he was pointing at the cup holders in his raft.

"Sodas," I said. "You thirsty?"

"Yeah," he said.

Hooray for William. I was instantly, overwhelmingly thirsty myself, and grateful for a getaway. "I'll get some." I hoisted myself out of the pool and headed for the pool house.

"I'll help," Luke offered, and before I could say I really didn't need any help getting sodas from the pool house fridge, he was out of the pool, dripping on the hot stone deck.

"Okay," I said. He followed me across the deck and into the pool house, where he closed the door behind us.

10

IT WAS DARK IN THERE UNTIL I opened the refrigerator door. I grabbed two Sprites and handed them to Luke, but didn't look him in the face. It's not the first time he'd been in the pool house; we have parties all the time and anyway I could see his and William's T-shirts on the bed in one of the rooms, the one to my right. But there we were, in the pool house, dripping wet, alone together.

"You want a towel?" I asked, going quickly around him, trying not to look at his flat stomach and tan chest on my way to turning on all the lights and opening the closet. When did he get arm muscles? I flung a towel back toward him. He caught it on top of his soda cans.

"Phoebe," he said.

I took a breath and forced myself to look up at him. Water was dripping off his hair.

"Yeah?"

He took a deep breath, too, and looked at his feet. "So,

uh, what's going on?"

My mouth opened but nothing came out. Going on? With me and him? Me and Kirstyn? My family? "I honestly have no idea," I whispered.

He smiled, frowned, then smiled again, so quickly that if I hadn't been staring at his face I'd definitely have missed the frown.

"What?" I asked, echo-smiling.

"Nothing, just . . ." He bit his lower lip. "I just know exactly what you mean."

"You do?"

"No." When I squinted at him, he smiled again. "Not exactly, I guess, I mean, but yeah. It's weird, isn't it?"

"What?" I tried to keep smiling, but it was a challenge.

"Everything," he said.

"Yeah," I said. Okay, so here's the thing. He really is incredibly cute. He's fun and hot and maybe Kirstyn was right about me liking him again, and I had just been in denial.

How intense and black are his eyes? Were they always like that?

He isn't the clingy little mama's boy he was when we were five, I thought, but hello, I'm not in a little pink dress anymore, either. And the way I acted to him the first week of seventh grade was so long ago, I was probably remembering it all wrong anyway. Maybe I hadn't been as much of a jerk as I thought. Maybe he'd forgotten, or decided we had all grown up a lot and forgiven me.

There was really nothing stopping us from hooking up, since that's what we clearly both wanted to do.

Well, anything other than the fact that my best friend would think I was crazy, and an idiot, and a loser. But maybe she would never know anyway.

He took a step toward me. We had only kissed a few times, back when we went out in sixth grade, and all those kisses (other than the last one) were in front of everybody, at those dumb parties we used to have. Still, I could remember how soft his lips were, how lightly they brushed mine, so different from gross Dylan Baker at camp with his gross tongue. Ew, I couldn't even think about *him* without gagging; I don't care how tall he was—yuck. So what if Luke is only my height, and wears Old Navy clothes, and maybe doesn't shave at all yet, and his father is friends with my father and we've known each other forever?

Right there in my pool house, on a perfect warm May day, in my best Calvin Klein bathing suit and him in just shorts, smiling at me like that . . . it did not seem babyish and boring to think about kissing him again. The opposite, actually.

"I was wondering," Luke said.

I just waited. I didn't want to mess him up, in case he had it kind of planned out or something.

"Do you have any chips in here?" he asked.

"Chips?"

"I'm starving."

"Oh," I said. "You want some, some what?"

"Whatever, pretzels. Doritos. Remember one time you had those orange things, the crunchy ones?"

"Yeah," I said. I opened the cabinet with all the snack food. "Take whatever you want." If this was his introduction to asking me out, I was not hugely impressed. "What else were you, um, going to ask? Or say? Or whatever?"

"Nothing," he said. "I just . . . I'm just a little . . . I'm always hungry lately." He shrugged apologetically.

"You're hungry," I said.

"Is that okay? You seem, kind of, annoyed."

"No, not at all," I said, completely annoyed. "Take as much as you want." *You immature puppy. You want chips? That's what you want? Take them. I don't know why you had to look all cute and bashful, if all you wanted was a snack.* But I didn't say any of that. I just pointed at the well-stocked shelves.

"Okay. Thanks." He put down the sodas and the towel and came to check out what was in there. *Great. Fine. Take some chips. What do I care? I had come in for a soda, nothing more. I've got bigger stuff to deal with than snacks, or hungry boys. Take every bag of chips in the whole cabinet, for all I care.*

I held the door handle and he leaned forward to choose what he liked from the freaking buffet of chip choices. "Um," he said.

I let out my breath, maybe impatiently. I was starting to

get cold in there, waiting for him to choose his damned snack. He stood up, and his face was moving toward mine before my mind registered what he was doing.

In fact, I wasn't sure what was happening until his lips touched mine.

11

IT CAN'T HAVE BEEN MORE THAN a minute before Gosia called my name. I pulled my face reluctantly back from Luke's but didn't answer her. He blinked twice at me when she yelled my name again. His body was so much warmer than mine, and his mouth tasted so good.

"What!" I yelled.

"Dinnertime," Gosia yelled, right outside the pool house door.

Luke turned away.

"Okay, okay," I yelled, and then whispered, "Sorry."

"No, that's . . ." He went into the changing room and grabbed his stuff and William's. "We should . . ." he said.

"Yeah," I agreed, and realized I wasn't sure what I was agreeing with, so I added, "I mean . . ."

"Mm-hmm," he said, eyes on the floor, and wiggled past me to get to the door. I followed him but it turns out he wasn't holding it open for me so it kind of slammed in my face. By the time I got out, he was diving into the pool, the pile of clothes dumped on the side. Gosia gave me a quizzical look. I shrugged and looked back at the pool to see Luke swimming fast to the shallow end. He climbed out and said to William, "Let's go."

William looked back and forth between me and Luke as he scrambled out of the pool and into his clothes. "I'll just call my mom to pick us . . ."

"Use your cell," Luke said. "They're having dinner. Come on."

"If you . . ." I started.

"Thanks for . . ." Luke looked up at me for a second. "I mean, thanks." His cheeks turned deep red on the sides. He grabbed William by his damp T-shirt and pushed him. "Their dinner is ready!"

"Dude," William said with a laugh in his voice. "Chill!"

I turned to shrug at Gosia, expecting her to grin at me knowingly. She was pale and serious. "Dinnertime," she said, and walked toward the back door.

Following her inside, I grabbed a sweatshirt off a hook and turned to go to the kitchen, but nobody was there. He kissed me, I was thinking. Gosia was holding open the dining room door, looking down at her ballet flats. Beyond her, my sisters and my parents were all sitting at the dining room table.

I almost asked what we were doing, if company was coming—but their quietness erased the smile off my freshly

kissed lips. I squeezed into my chair next to Allison without pulling it out first.

There were plates of salad in front of us all. Nobody
had touched a fork. I didn't know where to look.

"For this and for so much else," Mom quietly said, "we
are very grateful."

It's how we always used to start meals when I was
younger. It was Daddy's thing, that we should have
moments of gratitude before meals and other rituals, too.
Daddy likes rituals. The first Saturday every month he goes
at 6 A.M. to give out food at the homeless shelter; at least
twice a year he makes us gather up all the stuff we don't
wear anymore and he brings it to the Salvation Army; every
fifty-six days he gives blood at the blood bank. When he
kisses us good night he says, "Tomorrow is the first day of
the rest of your life." Or he used to. I don't know if he still
does; maybe after I'm sleeping he comes in and kisses my
forehead. We hadn't started a meal with "For this and for
so much else" in a long time.

He smiled slightly at Mom, who was grinding pepper
on her salad.

We all abruptly tried to eat. I did some cutting but
when I got mesclun leaves into my mouth they felt like play
food: rubber, unswallowable.

Mom put down her fork and knife. "I was fired today,"
she said.

We all put down our silverware, too, and looked at her

with our hands under the table.

She took a deep breath. Her eyes were clear and her voice was steady. "What happened is, I have been doing research for years on a pharmaceutical company named Galen. You might have heard me mention it?"

We nodded.

Mom continued, "It's a small company, but well capitalized, very exciting stuff in the pipeline. Well, it ran into some snags this week and I lost a lot of money on it. A lot of money. I still think I was right to take an aggressive position on it. I still say you'll see it hit twenty-five or even thirty before year-end. But it's not enough to be right. You have to be right at the right time." She forced a small smile. "Because the market can stay irrational longer than you can stay solvent."

I glanced at my sisters to see if this made any sense to them. It was hard to tell. They were focusing on Mom with serious faces so that's what I did, too.

"But I think this can be remedied," Mom said. "I'm setting up a meeting with the principals, and I think I can make a case to them. Everything is going to be okay. I don't want you girls to worry."

My sisters nodded so I nodded, too.

"I would like this all to be kept as private as possible," Mom continued.

"Of course," Quinn said immediately.

"Absolutely," Allison said.

"*Absonitely,*" I said, not wanting to copy but changing to "definitely" mid-word, too late.

Mom smiled at me. "Thanks. So, how was everybody else's day? Anything interesting happen?"

My sisters shook their heads so I shook mine, too, and then Gosia came in with turkey and rice and broccoli, which we all forced down as quickly as possible. I didn't think it was the right time to share the fact that only a few minutes earlier, I had been making out in the pool house. Although that certainly qualified as interesting, I was pretty sure it wasn't what Mom meant. I felt like I had to tell somebody, and almost said something to Allison on our way upstairs. But then I didn't. She and Quinn were both being so quiet, I had to be, too.

They each went to their own bedrooms and quietly closed their doors. I stood in my doorway for a minute, thinking we should really be clumped together on one of our beds, talking about what just happened. But when neither of their doors opened, I closed mine, too, and went to sit alone on my bed.

I wasn't sure what to think about. It was beyond weird to have so much happen and then not talk about it with my sisters at all.

Well, I decided, maybe it's good to have private stuff. I could deal with this whole Mom thing without their help. Not that there was anything particular for *me* to deal with. She'd work it out, she'd said. Of course she would. So nothing even to think about, there.

Which left the Luke thing.

How was I going to keep that to myself?

Well, I thought, why should I cheapen what happened by blurting it out all over the place? It's not like Quinn and Allison told me every time they kissed a boy. They totally never did! So I didn't have to tell anybody, either. It could just stay private, between me and Luke. That was way more romantic, anyway. So I resolved to keep (and enjoy keeping) the secret of kissing Luke to myself, forever.

12

"SO, YEAH, WE MADE OUT," I heard myself announcing. Behind us the grandfather clock chimed twice. I wasn't tired at all, though I did wish we could go back upstairs to Kirstyn's room and go to bed. I already regretted breaking my vow of secrecy.

But how do you not tell your best friends you kissed your ex? Especially when you are so busy not telling them everything else, something has to be let out.

"I knew it," Kirstyn said, shaking her head. "Didn't I tell you she liked Luke?"

"You did," Gabrielle whispered.

"I don't," I insisted, thinking, *Wait, do I? No, no I don't. I can't. We're friends, just friends. Friends who kissed two days ago. That's all. I don't want more, I don't need more.* The last thing I needed was complications. "I totally don't."

"Oh." Gabrielle made a face at Kirstyn, who laughed behind her hand.

"I was horny," I said, choosing Gabrielle's favorite word.

"You?" Gabrielle asked.

"You're not the only one who gets horny." I shrugged, trying to act as casual about it as I was trying to feel. "No big deal. So what, we made out. It wasn't the first time."

Maybe it won't be the last. No. Don't think about that.

"So you were just using him?" Kirstyn asked.

I wasn't sure what to answer, what she wanted me to say. I gathered the blanket around me tighter. "I guess," I said.

"Why not?" Gabrielle asked.

The flashlight in the middle of our tight huddle, pointed up at the coffered ceiling of the formal living room of Kirstyn's house, dimmed a little. It was Kirstyn's way of getting back at her parents: After they are snoring between their thousand-thread-count sheets, Kirstyn goes into the off-limits rooms of her house. She's been doing it all year. She doesn't eat or smoke or do drugs or have sex or anything while she's in there, and she doesn't sit on the couches or chairs because her butt would indent the down-filled cushions and she might get caught. She just goes in and sits there, on the floor, where she isn't allowed to be. And when we sleep over, we sit there with her. When the sky begins to brighten we have to back out of the rooms, rubbing away traces of our footprints from the silk rugs. But while we're in there, we lean toward one another and whisper secrets, or away from one another to think. It feels naughty, weird, and boring, all at the same time.

So that's what we were doing, leaning back, and my butt was starting to itch. I was wishing I could sit on the couch a few inches away that looked so soft and inviting.

"You were that horny?" Kirstyn asked.

I shrugged. It seemed like the simplest way to explain. I mean, I wasn't going out with Luke. He hadn't asked me out or anything—afterward, or since then. He'd had plenty of chances during the day in school.

"You know," I said, "It's not like it has to be true love or something. I mean, please. Right?"

"Absolutely," Gabrielle said, taking a big gulp from her water bottle. "We're way too young for love. We gotta just mess around awhile."

I nodded. "As you always say, Kirstyn, when we're in high school we'll do whatever we want with whichever guys we want. But right now these are the guys available and sometimes, you know, you kiss what you got!"

"Well, can't argue with that!" Kirstyn whispered, and we rocked back and forth, trying to hold in our laughs. When we had ourselves under control, Kirstyn said, "It's kind of perfect, really, because he's obviously willing, and it's not like you have somebody from camp to fall back on . . ." She gestured toward Gabrielle, whose camp boyfriend is sixteen. "So, why not use him?"

"Yeah," I said, although that was not really it. "I mean,

it's not like . . . I mean, we're friends."

"Whatever," Gabrielle said. "They're buddies. They both get horny so who cares. You use each other, nobody gets hurt. It doesn't have to be anything romantic."

"Right," I agreed. She was just agreeing with what I said. So why was my stomach a fist?

"Absolutely," Kirstyn said.

At least she wasn't angry at me like I thought she might be, after I swore up and down I didn't like Luke and then went ahead and made out with him.

"I mean, you don't want to be a slut or anything," Kirstyn added. "But . . ."

The flashlight died. We all sat there for another minute until Kirstyn whispered, "Let's go up to my room." We backed out, with Kirstyn going last so she could smudge over our footprints. Kirstyn's house has like thirty rooms but she's only ever supposed to go in three: her room, the kitchen, and the media room. We tiptoed up the stairs behind her.

Kirstyn turned on her TV and we all sat on her bed for a while, watching, getting dozy. After a while, Kirstyn hit mute. "Did I tell you Justin and I were texting like all night last night?"

"No," Gabrielle and I both said.

"I told him I was busy tonight, though," she said. "Hard to get, you know."

We both nodded.

"Oh, so anyway, I was talking about the party with my mom and we think, I mean, I'm really glad we're doing it."

I smiled at her. She looked kind of sad. I hadn't realized it but maybe she was feeling left out, that I had made out with Luke. I didn't want her to feel like Gabrielle and I were all coupled up suddenly and she wasn't. "Yeah, me, too," I whispered. "We're so lucky, the five of us . . ."

Kirstyn looked at me like I had lost my mind. "I meant because of how we're growing apart."

"Who?" I asked.

"The five of us," she said, and looked to Gabrielle for confirmation. "Zhara and Ann are great, you know I love them to death, but Zhara is just so serious and wonky, like, have a little fun, you know? And Ann, I mean, she is just more awkward by the day. And could somebody tell her to count a calorie? I don't want to be mean, but she is seriously spreading out. Right?"

Gabrielle shrugged. "They're just a little boring. Not their fault, but . . ."

"You think Zhara is really no fun?" I asked. "She's just . . . she's like the kind of funny you have to be standing right next to her to get, I think."

Gabrielle nodded. "You may be right. Maybe I need to stand right next to her more."

"Yeah," I said. "Don't you think? And Ann, I mean, I know she's kind of going through a stage of overly deep and down, but . . ."

"Ugh," Kirstyn said. "She's such a wet blanket."

"But . . ."

"Please!" She rolled her eyes. "I swear, you're getting almost as drippy as Ann lately. Lighten up, would you?" She smiled, but it was not a happy smile, and gave me what I think was supposed to be a playful kick. It hit me kind of off-balance though, and I fell off her bed.

It was one of those make-a-choice moments I sometimes have with Kirstyn, I could feel it—if I didn't want her to think I was a wonky, serious loser myself, I needed to come up with a jokey, light comment: *Kick me out of your bed, why don't you?* But as those words passed through my head and almost fell out of my mouth, they got stuck. Was she kicking me out? Why? *Lighten up,* I yelled silently at myself, but I couldn't lighten. I smacked a smile onto my mouth but couldn't manage a jokey comeback; I didn't trust my voice to be steady.

What was wrong with me?

I just sat there smiling psychotically at them. They were starting to look a little worried. I tried to pull the smile down a notch but it was stuck. Kirstyn and Gabrielle glanced at each other warily.

"Yeah," I finally forced myself to say. "I guess you're right. About them. About Zhara and Ann." I was seriously about one second from bursting into tears. I felt like such a low-life nasty traitor. The first rule is self-defense; I know I heard that somewhere, and I tried to convince myself that's all I was doing. Still, my teeth felt like they were rotting right in my head. "They are kind of . . . both . . ."

Kirstyn nodded and turned to me, her big blue eyes soft and gentle, like I was her stupid but beloved underprivileged cousin. "So I think it's pretty obvious to everybody that this party is really like a good-bye to our tight friendship, which is why I think it is so important to all of us, really. Don't you think so, Phoebe?"

I shrugged. I had thought everything was fine, that we were all still best friends, that we loved one another. When did all this happen, and did everybody know it except me? I tried to swallow.

We all just sat there for another few minutes, saying nothing, until Kirstyn said, "Anyway, it'll be an awesome party. I'm really looking forward to it. Aren't you?"

"Oh, absolutely," Gabrielle said. "Did you hear the soccer boys at lunch? Talking about getting a limo for it?"

"Yeah," I managed. "They sounded pretty into it."

"Oh, totally. Party of the year. Well, I gotta get some sleep," Gabrielle said. "I have a tennis match in the morning." She scooted down onto the air mattress. I turned to shrug at Kirstyn, because we always stay up until dawn at sleepovers.

"Yeah, let's go to sleep," Kirstyn said. She shut off the TV and snuggled down under her covers. I took the hint and got into my air-mattress-bed between them.

"You guys?" I whispered.

"*Shh,*" Kirstyn whispered back, and turned over.

When the sunrise finally came, I was the only one still awake. Usually at that point we are all in the kitchen eating Oreos and giggling.

I don't think I've ever felt lonelier.

13

I WALKED INTO THE ARCTIC BLAST of my house from the thick humidity outside and dropped my duffel. "Phoebe?" Mom called. I ventured into the kitchen. She usually works on Saturdays. Oh, yeah. It all came rushing back.

"Mom?"

She closed the refrigerator, a bottle of water in her hand. She was in sweaty running clothes. I watched her chug the water in quick gulps, and then yank the sweatband back off her hair.

"Hi," I said.

"Dress shopping," she answered.

"Huh?"

"For your party. Give me fifteen minutes and we'll go find something spectacular." She leaned toward me and I froze. Was there a Rice Krispie on my cheek from breakfast at Kirstyn's? But no, she was kissing the air near my face, weirdly. Before I could manage to pronounce okay, she was out of the kitchen, taking the stairs by twos up to her room.

I waited in the kitchen, looking out the bay window over the sink, past the pool and the tennis court in the backyard, to where some birds were flying low across the lawn. I think a teacher once said you can tell it's going to rain if the birds are flying low. Or maybe I dreamed that. It occurred to me that I could probably learn a lot if I ever listened in school. The sky was bright blue, so I must have dreamed it, I decided.

When Mom came down in jeans and a white T-shirt, her hair combed damp and her face as beautiful and sharp as always, I was guzzling a glass of orange juice. "You know that's pure sugar," she said.

"No wonder I like it," I said, putting it in the sink.

She laughed, bigger than normal, then sighed. "Ready?" I followed her out to the garage and got in the passenger seat of her Porsche. We drove without talking. She drives really fast but it still felt safe. The seat kind of hugged me, which was nice. I was kind of disappointed we got to the Neiman Marcus parking lot so fast.

As we walked through the store together, toward the juniors department, I watched people's heads turn. Everybody looks at her and she doesn't even notice. "Have fun last night?" she asked.

I shrugged. "Sure." *What if she asks me how things are going with my friends?* I thought. *Because, I mean, of course things are fine, just, I've been a little weird lately, no big deal.*

Or maybe somehow she'd figured out about Luke, that I'd kissed him again, or that I kind of liked him, or was using him, or even worse, was not. "Why do you want to know?" I asked her.

She looked at me funny. "Why do you sound like Allison all of a sudden?"

I laughed. "Ew. I don't know."

She laughed, too. Phew. We went the rest of the way without talking. At the juniors department, salesladies flocked around Mom, as they always do. They can just tell. I went one time with Ann and her mom and we couldn't get anybody to help us at all.

Mom explained that we needed a fabulous dress for my graduation party, so immediately all three salesladies, knowing the drill, fell all over one another to compliment my figure, my face, my eyes, my hair. I shrugged at Mom, who shrugged back. We knew the drill, too.

They showed us so many dresses my head was spinning, but Mom quickly said yes or no to each and then we went to the dressing room. "Socks, too," she reminded me. I peeled them off, remembering I had worn them yesterday and slept in them last night and they smelled a little bit like it. I shoved them under my jeans and pulled on the first dress.

"No," Mom said, and I whipped it off. I don't even think I looked at it.

About five or six dresses in, I saw the green one I had clipped a picture of from *Teen Vogue*. I pulled it carefully over my head and closed my eyes. She didn't say anything so I opened them. Her hands were over her mouth as she looked at me in the mirror.

"What?" I looked at myself, then looked away. I didn't want to look too closely, because I had imagined myself in this dress so many times it was kind of weird. Dancing with my friends, dancing with Luke, slow dancing with Luke, last dance of the party, with Luke's arms pulling me close to him . . . always, always, in this emerald green dress with the straps spread far apart on my shoulders. I waited for her no.

It didn't come.

I looked up again. She was blinking, staring at me in the mirror, her hands still over her mouth. Okay, look.

I slid my eyes over to my reflection, and there I stood, shoulders hunched but otherwise just as I had dared to imagine I might look in this beautiful dress, when I imagined it, alone and in my pajamas. Beautiful. I mean the dress, of course; it was as beautiful as it had looked in the magazine.

"You're beautiful, baby," my mother said.

I opened my mouth to joke, to disagree, to argue. But then I didn't, because the thing is, for the first time ever, I was. She was right. I looked beautiful.

I uncrossed my arms and let myself look at it, this beautiful girl in the mirror, in this deep green dress that fit her like it was designed for her, sculpted onto her, the same exact color of her eyes, matching and highlighting the slight curves of her body, straight as it was. She looked beautiful. And she was me. I met Mom's eyes and there were tears in them.

"Wow," she said. "That's your dress."

I nodded, touching the soft silk near my hips.

She closed her eyes and breathed deep. Her hand went again to her mouth as she swallowed. "Okay," she said softly. "Let's go. It doesn't need a single stitch."

I took it off and she hung it on the hanger while I put my regular clothes back on. When I had tied my shoes, I followed her and the dress, high on the hanger in front of her, to the checkout counter.

The woman smiled at us. "We just got that one in. Stunning, isn't it?"

"Stunning," my mother agreed, taking out her charge card and handing it over.

"You could be sisters," the lady said, moving smoothly and fluidly, whipping the card through the machine, shimmying a garment bag down over the dress. "You're too young to have such a magnificent daughter."

"She's my baby," Mom said. She snapped and unsnapped the silver closure on her wallet.

"No," the lady said, frowning at the machine. "You have more?"

"Three girls," Mom said.

"Lucky you," the lady said. "Sorry. I have to run your card again. This machine is so cranky."

"No problem," Mom said. Her hand tightened on her wallet.

"All as beautiful as this one?" the lady asked, still frowning.

Mom nodded. "Beautiful girls."

"Like their mama," the lady said, frowning even deeper. "I really apologize. Do you have another card? This temperamental machine . . ."

"Of course," Mom said, handing over another, then checking her watch.

"I really do apologize," the lady said. "This shouldn't take another second." She turned to me and smiled. Her teeth were yellow, I noticed. "Your prom?"

"Graduation," I said. "Eighth grade graduation."

"Oh, very sophisticated taste." She lifted her black framed glasses on their chain and peered down through them. "This is quite a dress for such a young girl."

"It was made for her," Mom said.

"You're very lucky," the lady said, flashing me a kind of evil look. "Aren't you?"

I shrugged and said, "Yeah, I guess."

"Would you mind hurrying please?" Mom asked. "We're in a bit of a rush."

"Yes, of course, only this card was rejected, too."

I was starting to sweat. "Never mind," I said to Mom.

Mom threw another card onto the counter. "Put it on this one." Her eyes were fire. The lady behind the counter stopped smiling and focused on typing in the numbers.

Her foot tapping, Mom rifled through her bag, then

checked her watch.

"This one is declined as well," the lady said, handing it cautiously across the counter.

Shaking her head, Mom tossed it into her bag and thrust another at the lady. "Here's my Neiman's card."

The lady smiled without showing her yellow teeth. I turned my back to her and leaned against the counter, waiting, listening to my mother's nails drumming impatiently. I glanced around quickly to make sure nobody from school was around.

"I'm sorry," the lady said.

Mom exhaled hard, holding her hand out for it.

"I apologize, the computer says they—I have to cut it."

"What are you talking about?" Mom demanded. The lady swiveled her screen around. Mom looked at it; I didn't. I was sinking down onto the floor. I heard scissors snipping plastic above my head. "That is the most ridiculous . . . give me your name." Mom was speaking quietly, clipped, in her most severe voice.

The lady spelled out her name and Mom entered it into her BlackBerry. The lady was apologizing, saying she was only doing her job, as Mom told her she was used to a different level of service.

"Let's just skip it," I said.

"I'll pay cash," Mom said, taking out her wallet. "How much is it?"

"Four forty, plus tax," the lady mumbled. "So that's . . ."

"I'll have to . . ." Mom stopped. I looked up. She was just standing there, holding her wallet and staring into space.

"Mom?"

She looked up at the ceiling, blinking.

"I don't even like that dress," I lied, standing up.

Mom shook her head. "We'll be back later, after I speak with your manager."

"Yes, ma'am," the lady said. "Of course." She looked up at me pityingly. I could've punched her.

Mom and I walked back out the way we had come. Her eyes were like lasers, straight ahead. I kept up the pace beside her. It wasn't easy; she was fast. I wished I could put my arm around her, tell her it was okay, tell her it didn't matter, but what could I do? I just tried to keep up.

Not saying the wrong thing is easier if you say nothing.

Near the door, I heard my name. Kirstyn and her mother were heading toward us, big smiles beaming. My mother grimaced, said the S-word quietly, the exact same word I was holding in. We both straightened up and smiled.

"Hey," I said to Kirstyn.

"Hi!" she said.

"Hi, girls!" her mother said. "Looking for dresses, I guess? Us, too." She patted her huge shiny pocketbook. "Kirstyn has a whole file of ideas clipped. This is so exciting, isn't it? Our babies are really growing up!"

Mom nodded at her.

"So did you find anything?"

Mom and I each shrugged a tiny bit. "Still thinking," I said.

"This place has really gone downhill," Mom said quietly.

"Oh," Kirstyn's mom frowned. "Maybe we should go someplace else."

Mom raised her eyebrows noncommittally and took a step toward the door. "Well . . ."

"Well, true, Kirstyn is shorter and, a bit, well, curvy in the behind, so they'd be looking at different things." She put her arm around Kirstyn and squeezed. "But I'd think Phoebe would be the easiest person to fit, no?"

"Fit is not the issue," Mom said tightly. "Everything looks stunning on her. It's just hard to decide and this place is so pretentious and airless it suffocates me. Let's go, Phoebe." She stalked out. I hurried after her.

She unlocked her car from fifty feet away with the key-chain thing, and slammed herself in. As I went around, got in, and buckled up, she sat stock still, staring ahead.

After a few minutes, I said, "Mom?"

She blinked twice. "Sorry," she whispered.

"For what?" I waved my hand in front of my face, like, *forget it*.

She shook her head. "We'll come back."

"I don't even—"

"Stop." She turned to me fiercely. "Yes you do, and you

should have it. This was . . . it isn't . . . there was just some confusion. My credit cards are all paid automatically online, so when the . . ."

"It's okay, Mom," I said. I just wanted her to stop. I didn't want to know. I wanted to just melt into the soft leather seat of her car and disappear.

"I can certainly afford to buy my daughter a dress for her . . ." She didn't finish. She turned and stared out the front window again. We just sat there for a few minutes and I was not saying one word. Her fingers were tight on the wheel, strangling it. I wished I could reach over and make them relax. I stayed as still as I could, tucking my own fingers under my thighs.

She took a quick sharp breath in through her nose and flicked the key in the ignition. We backed out of the spot and sped home, the long way, on the highway, very fast. When we got there, I unbuckled and got out but she didn't.

"You coming in?" I asked her.

She shook her head. "I'll be back later." She looked up at me.

I turned away. Her eyes looked too complex. I couldn't meet them.

"Okay," I said. "It's all good."

She shifted her eyes down and away.

"I mean . . ."

But by then she was peeling out, backward, down the driveway.

14

INSIDE, DADDY WAS SITTING IN his den watching baseball, grouching at the TV. He pried his eyes off the screen for maybe two seconds when I said hello. I wandered into the kitchen and slid open the wide drawer. After checking that nobody was coming, I pulled out the emergency money envelope. Four singles, nothing else. I put them back in, replaced the envelope, closed the drawer.

Taking the back stairs by twos, I went looking for Allison or Quinn, to tell them what had happened, see what they thought.

Allison was about to go out so she was in her room having her self-hate-fest first, trying stuff on and ripping it off, grunting that she was hideous. When I tried to compliment her she screamed at me and accused me of taking her white sweater, which I totally didn't, and anyway I thought it was supposed to be for both of us and in case it had somehow ended up in my bottom drawer, I had to lock her out of my room and lean against the door. Quinn was in her room studying the whole time until somebody beeped in the driveway and she sprinted out of the house. When I went by Allison's room a little later with the white sweater, she was already gone.

That's okay, though, I told myself. I'm not a baby. I can handle all this stuff on my own. I put the sweater on Allison's spring sweater shelf in her closet and quietly closed the door.

I had just settled down in front of the TV in the family room with a pint of Cookie Dough Dynamo and a spoon when my phone buzzed. I checked caller ID. It was Luke. I shut off the TV and waved my hands around like a lunatic before answering as cool as possible, "Hello?"

"Hello, this is Luke," he said.

"Hi." I ate a spoonful of ice cream. My mouth was burning up.

"Oh," he said. "So, um, Memorial Day?"

It was obviously a question but I had no clue what to answer. "Uh-huh?" is what I came up with.

"You going away?"

"I don't know," I said, downing another spoonful. "Is that next weekend?"

He laughed. "Wow, somebody spacier than I am. That's impressive."

"Thanks," I said. "I knew I'd impress somebody some-day." Youch, that had come out way flirtier than I'd intended. We both kind of breathed for a few seconds. I read the ice cream label. Holy fat content! Luke, you called me!

"Yeah," he finally said. "So are you? Going away?"

"Um, no," I said. "I don't think so. Nobody said anything about it to me, anyway. Not that that means anything. Ha ha ha!" *What is wrong with me?*

He laughed one *ha*. "Yeah, I hear you. I mean, good. I mean, I'm not either."

"Oh," I said. I swear he and I used to have normal conversations all the time, even when we were going out. Especially when we were going out. It was more like we were friends, like best friends, then. We played a lot of Stratego and Ping-Pong and laughed all the time. "What?" I asked.

"I didn't say anything."

"Oh," I said again, slapping myself on the forehead. "I thought, nothing."

Silence again. Think of something to say, Phoebe! How about, *Hey, remember when we kissed? Like less than a hundred hours ago?* "So anyway."

"So I was thinking," he said, "probably you don't want to so you can say no, no problem but I am probably going to be, you know, working in my mom's nursery? Repotting? And I was thinking if you felt like doing some transplanting there's like a million pots of orchids and they all have to be replanted, transplanted, but probably you don't want to which is fine," he said in one breath.

I replayed that whole thing in my head, twice, and when I finally got it, said, "Sounds like fun."

"Really?" he asked. "It's kind of a mess."

"I love dirt," I told him. "You know I do."

"Yeah. Just, I didn't know if you still did," he said.

He was right. We maybe didn't know each other so well anymore. "I do," I said. "I still do."

"Okay," he said. "Good. Great. So, then, it's a date. I mean, not a date. Not a date date."

I laughed or actually kind of brayed. Like a donkey. Unfortunately.

"I mean, or we could go to the movies, after. At the mall. If you want."

I smiled. If I want? "Which day?"

"Saturday. Okay? Week from today?"

"Great." We hung up and I picked up the remote and the ice cream and the spoon, thinking maybe my luck hadn't completely run out after all.

15

SUNDAY WAS GRAY AND GROSS OUT, much cooler than it had been. So much for the heat wave that fooled us into thinking summer had come early this year. Plus my sisters weren't home, Gosia had her day off, and mom was gone before I stumbled down for breakfast. Dad was at the counter, reading the paper, drinking his tea, made from the new stainless-steel teapot Mom had bought him—one with an out-pointing spout.

"Hiya, sweetheart," he said. He gave me a kiss on my forehead.

"Do you like that tea kettle?"

He looked, then shrugged. "Sure. Why?"

"Nothing."

"How about some omelets?"

He and I make killer omelets. "Yeah!" I said, and started getting out the ingredients. We make them loaded—cheese, sautéed onions and mushrooms, fresh herbs. I checked the herb drawer—yup, both dill and cilantro. Yum. Daddy had obviously planned ahead, stopping at the farmers' market Friday and done the only kind of shopping he likes to do. He flipped on the radio on his way to getting out our favorite omelet pan.

"I thought you were never gonna wake up," he complained, dancing his goofy Dad-dance with the pan in one hand and a whisk in the other. The secret, he always says, is whisking the eggs.

I toasted some fresh bread and whisked the eggs, while he scrubbed and chopped. When we finally sat down, after singing "Natural Woman" really loud together, the whisk and spatula as microphones, we had worked up a big enough appetite to eat most of what we'd made.

While we washed the dishes, he sprang it on me: "Hey, can I ask you a favor?"

"If you love me and I'm beautiful," I said.

"I love you and you're beautiful." He handed me the pan to dry.

"Yes, then."

"Come with me to bring in the Salvation Army bags."

I groaned. "I hate doing that."

"I know," he said. "But just think, you'll be doing good, and we'll work on our harmony."

I rolled my eyes. "We could use it."

"Yes, we could." He shut off the sink. "Great. Fifteen minutes?"

I groaned again and headed upstairs to get dressed.

We loaded up his car with about twenty bags, then got in and sang the whole way there. He sounded good. I am pretty tone-deaf. Luckily, neither one of us cared.

In the Salvation Army parking lot, I got a big gray bin and he loaded the bags into it, and we pushed it in, together. Up at the desk, while Daddy was telling the guy with the clipboard his estimate of what all that stuff was worth, I noticed that Quinn's jeans with the cool back pockets were on top of one of the bags. "Hey," I said. "I love these." I pulled them out of the bag and held them up to me. They looked like they might fit. "Can I keep these?"

"I guess so," Daddy said, not even looking. "Gosia just put in all the stuff you guys don't wear anymore."

I glanced over at the other bags. What other things were they giving away without asking me if I wanted them? One bag had some of Allison's shirts in it. I picked the ugly top one up, to see what was under it. The really cute purple one! I knelt down next to it, to find more treasures.

Somebody next to me started digging through another bag. I looked up. It was Bridget Burgess.

She looked at me like she was seeing a ghost. She had Allison's pink tank top in her hand.

I forced myself to smile and say hi.

"Hi," she said. "Are you taking those jeans?"

I looked at Quinn's jeans in my hand, scrunched up with Allison's purple shirt. "No. I mean, I am, but . . ."

"They're really cute," she said softly. "If you decide you don't want them, let me try them on, okay?"

I nodded, trying to think of how to explain that I wasn't actually shopping, I was donating, without sounding like a judgmental jerk and completely embarrassing her. And myself.

"There's some cute tanks over there, too," she said, pointing toward the back. Her fingers were long and very graceful, their rounded nails painted black. "Sometimes they have good stuff, sometimes just crap. Do you shop here a lot?"

"No," I said quickly.

"I didn't think so," she answered, lowering her heavily lined eyelids. "Though you do seem to have a little more, what? Individuality? Than the others. But still, I didn't figure you for thrift shop."

I shook my head and stood up next to Daddy. "No. I'm not—"

"Hi," Daddy said to Bridget, who was still kneeling on the floor, picking through our stuff. "You look familiar. Are you a friend of Phoebe's?"

She planted one long bony hand on the hip of her faded jeans. "We go to school together."

Daddy pulled his eyes away from her and asked me, "Aren't you going to introduce us?"

I died a little inside. How can he be so thick and embarrassing? "Bridget Burgess, this is Jed Avery, my father."

"Hi, Bridget," my father said, smiling. "Good to meet you."

Bridget looked at him steadily and said, "Hi, Jed Avery." Then she bent over the Neiman Marcus bag to her right and pulled out my yellow shorts that I was looking for just the other day. "Do you think these are cute or too short?"

"Too short," I said quickly. Just what I need is Bridget Burgess slinking around school in my favorite shorts.

"Really?" she asked, inspecting them. "Yeah, I guess you're right." She dropped my shorts disdainfully onto the pile. "Some of this stuff is beyond, huh?"

Daddy laughed. "I thought you loved those!"

"Daddy!" I balled up the jeans and purple shirt a little tighter in my fist. "Let's go. Come on."

"Are you buying those or no?" Bridget asked, standing up and pushing her long bangs out of her actually kind of beautiful almond-shaped eyes, then pointing at Quinn's jeans.

I couldn't even look at her anymore. What was I going to do? Explain? Buy the jeans we just donated? I shook my head and handed the jeans over to her, and the purple shirt, too.

"Really? Thanks!"

I waved my hand like don't mention it. Please don't mention it. And please don't be like every other suck-up in school and ask me about the party!

She didn't. She just said, "Later."

Heading straight to the door, I was trying my hardest not to turn back and yell at Bridget Burgess, *I don't shop here. I shop at Neiman Marcus. I am not like you!* I pushed through the door and went out into the gray drizzle. I tipped my face up to the sky and let the rain join the tears cruising down my face.

I was never like her, I thought, even before. *Bridget Burgess lives down on Maple Lane. I am not like her.*

The memory of our one playdate crashed around in my mind, despite all my years of practice, since that afternoon in third grade, at blocking it out. We had walked there alone after school. I had never walked home even with my sisters, so I was scared from the outset. Then we got to Bridget's house, there was a rusty bicycle on the patchy brown lawn next to some tires and some other junk, and a broken screen door she let slam after us when we went in. A huge amorphous mother overflowed a shredding upholstered chair in the living room, smoking cigarettes and coughing horribly. I felt like I had wandered into the opening scene of a scary movie. She barked at Bridget to get her a drink and Bridget said, I will never forget, "All right, all right, keep yer pants on." To her mother! I was only in third grade so I didn't know that was an expression, and the horror of the thought that if we didn't hurry and get her a drink, she might actually take off her pants for some reason made me feel like I was going to throw up.

We went into the kitchen and there were dirty dishes piled in the sink, on the counters, everywhere, and food out, unwrapped, even an open container of milk. Bridget asked me if I wanted a snack. Was there anything I wanted less? Turns out, in fact, yes there was: When I said no thanks, she said, okay let's go out back and I'll show you my pet, which ended up not being a mangy dog as I had feared, but a boa constrictor.

Bridget told me, while holding the snake up to my face so that it looked straight into my eyes, that a boa constrictor will squeeze its prey to death and then eat it, digesting it slowly over time, like for it to digest a whole human child might take more than a week. When I could get my voice working, I managed to remind Bridget that she was supposed to bring her mother a drink. She asked me to hold her snake for her while she got it.

I knew there was no way I was ever holding that snake, which had started licking its lips hungrily, threateningly, so I lied. I said I was allergic to snakes. "Really?" she asked, sounding unconvinced as always, and said she thought snakes were hypoallergenic. I told her, honestly this time, that I thought I might actually be getting hives, and maybe I should call my father to come get me. She sort of deflated then, like some of the air had been let out of her, so I said I was so sorry I should have asked if she had a pet snake beforehand and I would've taken my allergy medicine in the morning, oh, well. "Yeah," Bridget said, "maybe next time," and she let me use the phone and then she waited out front with me for my father. She looked really sad as we were waiting and said, "Sorry." I wasn't sure what she was apologizing for but I spotted my father's car making the turn onto Maple Lane so I smiled reassuringly and said, "Oh, don't worry about it."

The next day in school, Kirstyn came up to me in the playground. She was the princess of third grade, already tough and cute in equal portions, and she had never particularly singled me out before that moment. "So you're friends with Bridget Burgess?"

Gabrielle was on one side of Kirstyn, and Ann was on the other. Ann, who had been my best friend until not long before that. They were all staring at me, their tight little fists on their hips.

"No," I said. "I'm not."

"You had a playdate at her house yesterday after school," Kirstyn said.

"Yeah," I admitted, but then I made a choice—I was not getting lumped in with Bridget Burgess. I didn't even like her. I was *not* her friend. I knew even then that what I did in the next few seconds would affect the rest of the year at least—whether I'd get my name called in the first few or last at recess kickball; whether I'd be picked as a buddy on class trips or be left to hold hands with the teacher.

It barely even felt like a choice. "I went there," I said. "And it was disgusting!"

A shift in Kirstyn's eyes, almost imperceptible but not completely, told me I had chosen wisely. "Really?"

"Totally," I said. "Dirty, gross—she has a pet boa constrictor!"

"No!"

The three of them crowded around me, but not hulking anymore; eager, admiring, awed. "There was spoiled food everywhere!"

Out of the corner of my eye I could see Bridget, twirling her greasy hair around and around her long, thin index finger. I slid my eyes away. I hadn't said anything untrue, but I knew what I was doing. I just surprised myself by how good I was at it, and how awfully fun it felt to be mean.

"Ew!" the girls were all shrieking around me. I couldn't help it; I looked over again to where Bridget had been standing, but by then she was gone.

"You want to go to the far fence with us?" Kirstyn asked, and I knew I had passed the test. I was in.

That was the day the four of us started being best friends, and then, when I moved down the street from Kirstyn, she and I naturally bonded the closest, the tightest pair within the group. Zhara moved here two years later and was so cool and pretty it was obvious she'd be in with us, too. We were the ones at the center of things, not because of anything we did, so much. It's just who we were.

I am not like Bridget Burgess, I reminded myself, my hand on the cold wet door handle of my father's car.

"Get in, you nut!" He reached across the passenger seat and opened the door for me.

I slumped into my seat. Daddy turned on the warmer. "You okay?" He checked his mirrors and backed up slowly. "She seems nice, Bridget. Beautiful girl. Didn't you used to be friends with her?"

I shook my head. "Never."

We waited at the light to pull onto the main road. Even the roads are dirtier there than near us; litter lined the sides near the crumbling curbs. It gave me the creeps. I turned on the radio. Dad turned it off.

"I have to talk with you, sweetheart."

"What?"

He pulled onto the road and started driving. "Mom told me about yesterday, what happened at the store."

I looked out the window, watching the raindrops squiggle down over the reflection of my face.

"That must've been uncomfortable," he continued.

I shrugged, thinking, *Please don't talk about it! I don't want to know!*

"There was just a glitch at the bank," he continued. "Our checking account was overdrawn when Mom had to transfer—"

"I know!" I said. "She told me. It's fine!"

He flicked the blinker and I listened to its rhythmic

clicking. "I don't want you to worry."

"I'm not."

"There's nothing to worry about."

"That's why I'm not worried," I said. *Man, he can be so frigging irritating! Bridget Burgess beautiful? What? She's not even close to a pretty girl.*

"But, that said," Daddy said. He made the turn and the blinker clicked off. "We are going to have to be careful."

"Careful?"

"We're in a challenging economic situation right now, and I think you are old enough to be made aware of some of the ramifications of it."

When he starts talking like a thesaurus, I get a fever. The car, as big as it was, started to feel like it was closing in on me.

"With Mom's work situation," he said, even-voiced, "we are not going to be able to splurge on unnecessary luxuries like extravagant dresses."

"It's not unnecessary," I grumbled.

"A five-hundred-dollar dress? I beg to differ," he said.

"Four-forty, and it's not like I chose it for the price tag! Mom's the one who said I should get it, not me."

"I just think it's a little extreme to expect—"

"Everybody is wearing dresses, Daddy! You want me to go back to the Salvation Army and pick out some dirty old reject rag? Why is this all suddenly my fault?"

"Phoebe—"

"Forget it! Fine. I'll wear jeans to my graduation party. Happy?"

He swerved the car into the Food Emporium parking lot, yanked hard to the right to pull across two parking spots like a slash, and slammed on the brakes. I grabbed onto the door handle. He is normally a highly cautious, safe driver. I turned to ask him if he was crazy but I didn't have to because it was obvious that he was. There were practically flames shooting out of his eyes at me.

"No," he growled. "I am not happy. I am not happy at all. Your mother is going through probably the worst time of her life and are you thinking, *Gee, how can I be supportive of the woman who has given me everything I've ever wanted, as soon as it pops into my head? The woman who has worked her ass off all her life so that I can live in this cushy heaven with every desire instantly fulfilled?* No. Instead of thinking of her for a change, it's all about you! Four hundred forty dollars for a dress you'll wear once? At fourteen years old? And a sarcastic, snide mouth—*are you happy?*"

My mouth dropped open. Was he seriously mocking me?

"It hurts me," he went on. "It disgusts me that these are the values my kids have. To see my daughter pout and feel sorry for herself that she can't get any overpriced designer gown she pleases—are you kidding me?" He slammed the palm of his hand hard into the rim of the steering wheel. "Am I happy? That I am raising a spoiled brat? No, Phoebe, I am not happy. Not happy at all."

The windshield wipers were squeaking back and forth. The rain had stopped. He turned them off.

"Sorry," I mumbled, slumping farther down.

He took a deep breath and then another.

I started crying. "I don't care about the dress."

He twisted his hands on the steering wheel.

"You really think that I'm like that? A spoiled brat?"

"I'm sorry I snapped at you."

I shook my head. He hadn't said *No, sweetheart, of course I don't think you are a selfish, self-centered spoiled brat.* He was just sorry he let it out. I could feel myself shivering. I didn't care. I watched the raindrops chase one another down my window.

"It's going to be okay, Phoebe. We just all have to be . . . thoughtful."

I nodded. Thoughtful. "We're not, like, poor, though, right?"

He didn't say no right away, like I expected. I had been afraid he might laugh at the stupidity of that question. Suddenly I was afraid because he didn't. "I honestly don't know what's going to happen. I do know that right now we are not in any position to be spending thousands of dollars on this extravagant party you and your friends have cooked up."

I stared at the window, placing mental bets on the left raindrop to beat the one next to it. "So now you're canceling my party?"

"Phoebe," he said. "I'm sorry you're disappointed, but—"

"My graduation party?" I looked at him. He was totally serious. He tilted his head sideways, sympathetically. I felt my mouth drop open in disbelief.

"You can't!" I yelled. "It's all planned, the place, the DJ, the invitations! Everybody in the whole grade is looking forward to it. My friends are counting on me!"

"So am I," he whispered. He looked at me, narrowing his dark eyes. "So are we."

"Fine," I said, sinking down inside myself.

"Maybe we could have a party at home. A pool party—everybody could come over after graduation and—"

"No!" I shouted. I took a deep breath to calm myself down, so he wouldn't go off on me again. "Not gonna happen. Please don't."

He nodded. "I'll call Kirstyn's parents," he said quietly. "I'll just let them know we're sorry, but this isn't something we can do right now. I'm sure they'll understand."

"You said I could do this party," I grumbled. "You and Mom both said yes already! And now you want to call all my friends' parents and say, *Oops, sorry, we're poor*?"

"I don't think I'd put it quite that way," he said.

I shrugged, not looking at him. "Let me tell my friends. Okay?"

"I really think it's my job, not yours, Phoebe."

"Please?" I begged him. "Please. It's my party, my friends."

"Of course," he said. "But it's not your responsibility to—"

"Yes it is!" I yelled. "I'm part of this family, and I'm not a baby or a spoiled brat, Daddy, no matter what you think. You can at least let me, after you tell me I have to, whatever, do my share, can I please at least be given half a chance?"

"If you're sure you want to handle this on your own . . ."

"I am," I said, sounding more sure than I felt. "Please."

"Okay," he said again, staring out the front window. "Okay. I love you. You know that, right?"

I shrugged and turned away. My raindrop, the one on the left, had gotten stuck, clinging stubbornly to its spot on the glass, as the other one zigzagged down, down, down. I rested my hot forehead against the window and closed my eyes.

16

FIRST THING MONDAY MORNING, Ms. Alvarez knocked on my desk, where I was resting my head, and asked me for the draft of my graduation speech. I cleared my throat, stalling. I was so tired, my brain was in slow motion. *Think!* I had already said, Friday morning, that I was still working on it, not ready to show it yet, and she had told me to work on it over the weekend but not be such a perfectionist—after all, it was only a draft.

"Forgot to bring it in . . ." I managed, vowing silently to start working on it soon.

"Are you feeling ill?"

I tried to smile.

She bent close and asked, "That time of the month?"

I shrugged. What a nightmare, the mustachioed home-room teacher was hovering sympathetically, three inches from my face. Even worse, based on my unwilling sample whiff of her breath, she was a smoker. *Bleh!*

"I'll bring it in tomorrow, Ms. Alvarez."

"I'll look forward to reading it, dear," she murmured, and, thankfully, plodded back toward the front of the room. I sunk into my chair. Just what I need, on top of everything else—to write a speech summing up our middle school experience. Great. How about, *Everything was perfect until recently?*

At lunch we sat in our usual clump. All the other kids gathered closer than they needed to, pretending they weren't listening in for scraps of info about the party to then shoot around in rumors and wannabe insider gossip. The five of us leaned close to whisper. Our notebooks open, we nodded like a bunch of bobbleheads. I wasn't even sure what I was agreeing to. There was a buzz, a hum, under everything; I couldn't hear. Like I was looking through the wrong end of a telescope, my friends seemed strangely far away, though there they were, right beside me at the lunch table as always.

On our way outside, after smiling randomly at a couple of girls who complimented us as we passed, I saw a penny in the hallway. I lurched down to grab it, feeling hopeful for the first time all day that maybe I could get some luck back. Kirstyn grabbed my wrist. "Was that heads up?"

"What?"

"The penny. I think it was heads down."

"So?"

"That's bad luck."

"Find a penny, pick it up, and all the day you'll have good luck," I said. "There's nothing about heads up."

"Trust me." She still had a death lock on my wrist.

"Okay." I dropped the penny. "It's just a superstition anyway; it doesn't really work."

"If you say so," Kirstyn said, shaking her head sadly. "It's too late now. You picked it up. Bad luck."

I kicked the penny to the side of the hall.

"Hey, so are you coming to East Hampton with us this weekend?"

"Who's us?"

"Gabrielle's family. For their Memorial Day party. Earth to Phoebe! Didn't she ask you this morning?" She leaned into the heavy door to push it out. The sunlight smacked us and we both whipped out our sunglasses.

"No," I said, putting mine on. I still had to squint anyway.

"Well, I'm pretty sure she was going to." She looked at me. "Seriously. Don't worry."

"I'm not worried," I said. *How much do I hate it when people tell me not to worry?* "But, um, I just, the thing is . . ."

Luke's hand splayed out beside mine on the door. We all three walked through it together. Kirstyn elbowed me. I shrugged at her.

"What aren't you worried about?" Luke said.

"Ungh," I said back.

"Anything," Kirstyn said. "You know Phoebe. She

132

never worries about anything! Right, Phoebe?"

"I guess," I mumbled.

"So anyway, Luke," Kirstyn said, more cheerfully than I'd heard her speak to (or about) Luke in forever. "What are *you* doing Memorial Day weekend?"

He glanced at me. "Not much. How about you?"

Kirstyn smiled. "We're going out to East Hampton with Gabrielle's family. Have you been to their place out there?"

"No," he said. I felt kind of squashed between them as we headed up the hill in the bright sunshine.

"It's amazing. Her parents have fabulous Memorial Day parties."

"You're going to East Hampton?" Luke asked me.

"Um," I said. *No, I'm going with you to dig in dirt!*

Kirstyn threw her arm around me. "You gonna miss her?" she asked Luke flirtatiously.

He blinked twice and said, "No."

Kirstyn made a pout and yanked me away. "Come on, Phoebe."

I let her drag me away, toward the upper field, and didn't look back. I tried not to think of how familiar this feeling was, like I was one of those chocolate bunnies you get for Easter that, when you bite its ear, you find out the whole thing is hollow and shattering to bits in your fingers. Like I'd felt the last time Kirstyn led me away from Luke, the first full day of school last year. *Don't think about that! Ancient history!*

"I see what you mean," Kirstyn was saying. "I mean, he's still a little, you know, sweet, but he does have a very kissable mouth. You may as well make use of it, right?"

"Yeah," I said, crumbling, shattering, myself. "You know those hollow bunnies, and you bite them and you thought they were solid but they're not?"

"Gabrielle says the party is 'Hamptons casual,'" Kirstyn whispered. "But it's Saturday night so that definitely means dresses, don't you think?"

"I guess," I said. Maybe I hadn't said anything and just thought I had. Maybe I was suddenly getting deep and annoying. *Lighten up!*

"Do you have something new?"

"Yeah," I said, lightly, brightly, fakely. "I think so."

"While we were at Neiman's we got a few things."

"Great!"

She looked at me quizzically for a second. I had never noticed before how hard it is to strike the exact perfect level of light and bright. I shrugged casually and tipped my head up to the sun. "What did you get?"

"Oh! A bunch of cute things. I don't know what your mom meant—there were so many dresses! I tried on that green one, remember you clipped a picture from, I think, *Seventeen*? Green with straps up like this?"

"*Teen Vogue*," I whispered, trying to stay upright on grass that felt like it had started to liquefy.

"With the tight waist, full skirt—"

134

"I remember it," I managed to say.

"Well, it was right there, hanging by the desk! It's so cute but it makes me look a little dumpy, so we got that one and also a white with black—did you see that one? With the slit?"

I nodded, though I really couldn't tell what she was talking about anymore.

"Well, we brought them both home and . . ." I had completely stopped being able to hear her. She had my dress, and another, to choose from, hanging on the bar of her closet. And I was about to drown in the grass of the upper playground.

"Don't say anything to Zhara and Ann," I did catch.

"About what?"

"About this weekend. You know, going to Gabrielle's. We don't want them to feel bad or anything."

"Maybe she could invite them, too," I suggested, my voice far away from my mouth. "Maybe that could be fun, you know, all five of us, like last year. . . ."

Kirstyn rolled her eyes. "Sure. Last year was fine, but I mean, we're going into high school now. It's like, you know? They'd just feel uncomfortable, really. There are going to be all these boys there from the city, all Gabrielle's parents' friends' kids, including you-know-who."

"Miles?" I could hardly believe I was actually participating in the conversation. Miles was Gabrielle's boyfriend from camp. I'd never met him but I'd seen his picture.

That's it, keep up, I told myself. *Light, bright, casual—stay with it. You can do this.*

Kirstyn nodded. "With some of his buddies, so—who knows!" She squeezed me closer. "Make sure you don't bring your green-and-white bikini."

"The Calvin Klein?"

"It's so—middle school. No offense. But, you know? Don't you have some less, you know, *sporty* suits? These guys are in tenth grade. In case they come over during the day, you don't want to seem like a baby."

I shook my head. No, I didn't.

Kirstyn leaned close and whispered to me. "We have to make it seem like we hook up with tenth-grade boys all the time, no big deal. This is gonna be so great, don't you think?"

I nodded. Great. I turned around to scan the field but didn't see Luke anywhere. William was coming up the hill behind us. He smiled at me. I couldn't tell if it was a *you-made-out-with-my-best-friend-you-dog* smile, or a *my-best-friend-likes-you* smile, or just a *hello* smile. I smiled back, a *whatever* smile, I hoped, rather than a *trying-not-to-puke* smile.

"You okay?" Kirstyn whispered.

"Sure. All good." We were almost at the back fence, because it turned out we had kept walking. How odd everything was. Oh, hello, there's my hand, beside my head, waving to Gabrielle, Ann, and Zhara, who were sitting near the fence along with half the other girls in the school and some of the flirtier boys.

"You seem a little . . ."

"What?" I asked.

"Off."

She waved casually at a couple of seventh-grade girls from the track team who were watching us. They smiled big cute braces smiles, then huddled up to whisper to each other. William walked straight over to them.

"No, I'm on," I assured her.

"What?"

She scrunched her face; I smiled and shrugged. She bared her teeth at me. I shook my head; nothing caught. I showed her mine and she shook her head, too, then scrunched her nose at me again. It was kind of like a dance. Out of the corner of my eye I saw the girls shoving William on his shoulders. He laughed. They all looked like they were having a whole lot more fun than I was, that's for sure. I couldn't shake the peculiar feeling. I kept thinking, through a fog, *Wait—that's me, it's supposed to be me, the one in the middle of the fun. There's been an error, me here stressed, outside.*

"Um, Phoebe?" Kirstyn leaned close and whispered to me, "Listen. No big deal but I overheard my mother telling my father that your mother's check bounced. You know, for the party?"

"Bounced?" I asked.

"You know, when the bank screws something up so they think there's no money in your account and won't pay it? My dad was like, so just redeposit it, the bank must have screwed up."

She looked at me quizzically. I closed my eyes behind my sunglasses. "I'm sure it's nothing," I heard my mouth say, miles away.

"Obviously," Kirstyn said. "I just—"

"What?"

"Nothing. Just . . . if . . . never mind."

Bridget Burgess, sitting on the grass nearby, looked up at us with her hand shading her eyes. Her face was a mask, no expression; she was wearing Allison's purple top and my yellow shorts. Kirstyn turned to me and whispered, "If she dressed less tacky, it's weird but I think Bridget Burgess would actually be kind of cool-looking. Don't you? In a trashy-cool way?"

All I could manage was a shrug.

"Anyway," Kirstyn whispered, linking her arm through mine. "My mom is finally picking up the invitation proofs today. I can't wait to see."

"Mmm," I said.

"She said she'll get two, one for you to bring home, too, after she picks us up from track. Okay? Won't it be fun if we have tenth-grade boyfriends at our party? I mean, you promised it would be great, but seriously. Right?"

"Yeah," I said, plopping down onto the grass between

Zhara and Gabrielle. My head was spinning.

"What?" Ann asked.

"Nothing," Kirstyn said.

Ann frowned and picked some grass. I knew just how she felt but there was nothing I could do to help, because right then Gabrielle stood up and yanked Kirstyn by the belt loop and said she had to ask her something.

They stood a few feet away and I saw them trying not to look at me as they whispered. I tugged at the grass myself until the bell rang ending lunch.

Kirstyn, sweet and apologetic, grabbed my arm to walk down the hill, whispering, "I'm so sorry, Phoebe—I totally messed up. Don't be mad at Gabrielle. She's totally sorry and so embarrassed but it turns out her parents are limiting her so unfairly for the weekend because her brother is coming with friends from college."

Gabrielle caught up with us. "I'm so sorry," she whispered. "I really wanted you to come. . . ."

I managed to smile. "Oh, of course," I said. "I mean, no problem. I totally understand."

At our lockers, Kirstyn whispered, "Are you mad?"

"Not at all," I answered. "I don't really care, to be honest." Because, really, I didn't. I didn't care about anything, it turned out. If I could feel anything, I might have felt surprised to feel nothing.

"It has nothing to do with you," Kirstyn assured me. "Don't worry."

If one more person tells me not to worry this month I may have to kick them in the teeth, I thought, but I just said, "I know. I'm not worried." Clearly it had nothing to do with me. None of it did. I had lost track of myself somewhere. Who this girl was, walking beside Kirstyn down the hill, not being invited, not allowed to have her graduation dress or even a party, frowning in the sharp May sun—I had no idea. She wasn't me, obviously. I barely recognized her.

"You okay?" Kirstyn asked me. If there was a tiny little gloat under Kirstyn's sweet embarrassment, I tried to ignore it.

"All good," the girl beside her, who she thought was me, said.

17

I KNOCKED ON QUINN'S DOOR and waited, because she said to hold on. She opened it a crack and looked out at me. "What's up?"

"Not much. You?" I squinted at her. She looked different somehow. How?

"All good," she answered. I wondered if she meant it more than I did, lately. "How about you?" She opened her door and I followed her into her room, all reds and purples, with piles of books, pens, and papers everywhere.

"I'm good," I told her. "Anything new with Mom and all that?"

"Why?" She checked her reflection in the mirror and wiped under her eyes. That was it—her eyeliner was smudged. Had she been crying? Quinn?

"Just wondering," I said. The invitation proof I'd been holding felt too conspicuous; I dropped it on top of a rickety pile on Quinn's desk. "So?"

Quinn shrugged. "She's meeting with the lawyer a lot, and not going to the office, obviously. I think they postponed her meeting. She's been in the study all day, going through her files, preparing."

"Oh." I picked up a pink eraser and rubbed it against my palm. Wouldn't it be cool if you could just erase yourself, sometimes? "Well, I gotta go write my graduation speech," I said.

"Need help with that?"

"No, I got it," I said, trading the eraser for the proof. "I'll be fine. It'll be fine." I had my hand on the doorknob and one foot in the hall when I asked, "Hey, Quinn? If I wanted to get some money out of the bank, how would I do that?"

"Why?"

"I was just thinking—"

Something crashed into Quinn's window. Quinn and I both jumped. Before I could ask her if she thought a bird had smashed to its death, Quinn had run to the window and opened it.

"Get in, you idiot," she said, I thought to the dying bird. But no.

Allison crawled in, off the roof.

"Where the hell were you?" Quinn demanded in her hoarse low voice. I just stood there with my mouth hanging open. "Do you know what I—"

"We missed the train," Allison explained, panting. "I saw her car so I . . . what are you doing in here?" she asked me.

"I came in through the door," I said. "Did you cut school?"

Allison shot Quinn a look, then sighed. "I went into the city with Roxie."

"The city? By yourselves? Why?"

"To become fashion models."

"What?" I blinked twice. "No, really, why did you . . ."

"Thanks for the vote of confidence." Allison shook her head. "Ugh. Don't even ask. You do a friend a favor . . . and end up having your picture taken by a bunch of freaks."

"You had *your* picture taken?" Quinn asked her. That's what she was surprised about? Not that brainiac control-freak Allison had cut school and gone into the city with her crazy new best friend Roxanne—but that she'd had her picture taken? "You said only she—"

"I had to sign the thing, to sit in the room with her," Allison said. "What a joke: Three hundred girls, all as gorgeous as Roxie, and then me. Ugh. I think I just bruised my palm, climbing up here. What are you guys doing?"

"Phoebe needs money."

"For what?" Allison asked, inspecting her palm.

"I don't know," Quinn said. They both turned and stared at me.

"Mom's check bounced," I explained.

"What check?" Allison's eyes darted to Quinn, her bruised palm forgotten.

"To Kirstyn's mom," I whispered. "She's redepositing

it because, she figures, the bank messed up. So it's probably no big deal but . . ."

Quinn closed her eyes and breathed slowly. "It'll just bounce again, and Kirstyn's mother will call Mom."

"When?"

"I don't know," Quinn said. "When did it bounce?"

I shrugged. "Kirstyn told me about it this morning."

"We have a few days at best," Quinn muttered, figuring. "What was the check for?"

"Six hundred dollars," I whispered, sinking down onto Quinn's rumpled bed.

Quinn grimaced. "I mean, why was Mom writing her a check?"

"Oh," I said. "For my graduation party."

"You were supposed to get out of that!" Allison said. "Daddy told Mom—"

"How did you know?"

Allison shrugged. "Baby monitor."

"Right. Okay. But, see, I was thinking—instead of pulling out of the party, I could use my own money."

"Phoebe," Quinn objected. "That's for college. They'll never let you."

I grabbed the invitation off Quinn's desk and thrust it toward them. They both scanned it, their eyes moving around it, taking in the yellow paper with pink overlay, the perfect font, and around and around the edges, where our five names encircled the whole thing, linked in an unbroken chain.

"I can't just quit."

When they raised their eyes back up to mine, first Allison and then Quinn, I could tell they both got it, they knew.

"Mom doesn't want anybody to know our business anyway," Allison said, then added quietly, "Baby monitor."

"And why would she? I don't want to be a spoiled brat," I whispered. "But what am I supposed to do, realistically? I already committed; they said yes before they said no. And now, it's the biggest party of the year. Everybody's excited. There are rumors swirling—who's invited, who's not . . . People are totally kissing up to us trying to score invitations, even though we're inviting everybody. . . ."

"The whole grade?" Allison asked. "Why?"

I shook my head and picked up a pad of Post-its from Quinn's overflowing desk. "Because, I don't know, I thought I was, like, the mayor of the school and insisted we should. And now the only one in the known universe *not* coming is *me*."

"The known universe?" Allison repeated sarcastically. "Please."

"Seriously," I insisted. "I heard one girl saying she heard what's-his-name from the TV show with the football team? He's supposedly coming."

"The one with the cheekbones?" Allison asked.

"Yes! I mean, he's totally not. I don't think. But maybe Gabrielle's dad asked him. He's like the head of some . . . I don't know! It's crazy. This party is all anybody is talking about. So am I really supposed to just be like, *Oh, sorry,*

145

changed my mind, count me out?"

"Well, obviously you can't do that," Quinn said, taking the Post-it pad away from me. Without realizing it, I had pulled off like fifty of the sheets and let them scatter.

"Right," I said, kneeling down on the rug to collect the dropped Post-its. "So I'm thinking if I could just take out my own money, which I would totally earn back before college, somehow—but then I could call Kirstyn and say something like the bank is having a computer glitch and here's cash instead. Otherwise, Kirstyn's mom is going to call."

"We'll intercept," Allison said, picking up Post-its with me.

"She has their cell numbers, too," I told her.

Quinn took the papers from us and shoved them onto the already mountainous piles on her desk. She sighed heavily and raised her eyes to mine. "Maybe you should just confide in Kirstyn what's happening. She's your best friend."

"Are you kidding me?" I shrieked. "No way would I tell Kirstyn. How would that even help? What's she supposed to do, pay my share? Come on."

"She definitely can't tell Kirstyn!" Allison agreed. "Quinn!"

"I know it's hard," Quinn said. "But your friends love you, they—"

"No. Not anymore." I could feel tears starting behind

my eyes. "They don't. Something happened."

"*Shh.* Come in the closet," Quinn said. We followed her across her room. Unlike Allison's, Quinn's closet was a tumbling mess. She shoved some piles over and we all sat down on whatever was there—sweaters, sweatpants, sports equipment, books, shoes.

"What happened, Phoebe?" Allison asked.

"I don't know," I whispered, collecting myself. "Okay. Gabrielle was planning to invite me and Kirstyn to her house in East Hampton this weekend, and I was all like oh, great, even though I was supposed to get together with Luke Saturday—"

"Luke Stoddard?" Quinn asked. "You're back together?"

"Yeah, but I blew him off when Kirstyn said I was invited to Gabrielle's."

"You dumped him?" Allison asked. "Again?"

I nodded. "But then Gabrielle cancelled me."

"No way!" Allison said, horrified.

"Yeah."

"Why?" Quinn asked.

I shrugged. "She said her parents were being so annoying, not letting her invite as many people as last year. Remember when I went?"

"Oh, yeah," Allison said. "It was a total mansion, right? Oceanfront, servants, live band . . . weren't there violinists?"

"Up the steps," I said. "Yeah. She was all, 'so sorry,

please don't hate me' and I was like, 'no, no, I understand, no problem,' even though I was like, hello, I just dumped the boy I might seriously love because I thought it was more important to be with my friends and now he totally hates me. Fine, whatever. If you can only take one guest and you asked Kirstyn first, fine. But then, here's the bad part—"

"That wasn't the bad part?" Allison asked, leaning close, her thick eyebrows scrunched together in concern.

I shook my head sadly. "Zhara let it slip at the lockers after seventh that she's going to Gabrielle's this weekend, too."

Allison gasped. Quinn shook her head. They couldn't believe what a loser I was, suddenly, either.

"What did you do wrong?" Allison asked.

Anybody else, I'd be so mad and surprised if they asked that. But Allison really meant it in a helpful way, I could tell. She is nasty to me plenty, but right then her gray eyes were soft and I could tell she was mostly surprised. I'd never had friend problems before.

"I don't know," I said honestly. "I keep trying to figure it out. Maybe because I started liking Luke again? Or maybe I've been too stressed? I swear I didn't do anything so awful that they'd . . . You don't think they know, do you? About Mom?"

"No," Quinn said. "How would they?"

"Definitely not," Allison quickly agreed. "We've all

kept it completely secret. It has to be something else." She looked me up and down, appraisingly. "I don't know. You're still cute. But that sounds bad, Phoebe, it does."

I nodded. "And now, if they find out we can't afford the party . . ."

"We can afford it," Allison said. "It's just a temporary cash flow issue."

"A what?" I asked.

Allison shrugged. "Baby monitor."

"Whatever," I said. "But, so anyway, I was just thinking maybe if I could just get some of my money out of the bank . . ."

"Never gonna happen," Quinn whispered.

"I'll lend you some," Allison said, her lower jaw thrusting forward angrily at Quinn. "We'll get it."

"It's thousands," Quinn told her. "It's not just this couple of hundred. That's the *deposit*. You think you have thousands wadded up in old pocketbooks or something, Allison?"

"No," she said. "But her friends are dumping her! She can't call them up and say on top of whatever else, now I'm also poor! Don't you even care?"

"Yeah," Quinn whispered back, just as pissed. "I do. But what are you planning to do, just waltz on into the bank by yourselves and demand your money? Don't you think Mom or Daddy would have to get it for you? Or even if you managed to withdraw it yourselves, don't you see that you'd get caught eventually? And what will you say to them, then, when they're doing everything they can to keep a roof over our heads? 'We used our college money because we don't want Phoebe to be embarrassed in front of her lousy friends who don't even like her anyway'?"

My mouth dropped open and so did Allison's.

Quinn turned to me. "No offense."

"Some taken," I managed. Hard to believe these were the people on *my* side. "You know what? Never mind." I stood up.

Quinn yanked at my hand. "Sit down, Phoebe."

"No." I opened the closet door.

"Don't be a baby," Allison said. "Come on. We're trying to help you."

"I'm not a baby. You just treat me like one. But I'm not. And I don't need your help. I came in here to ask a simple question—do you know how I can access my money in the bank. The answer is no, you don't know. Fine. I'm not whining or crying or asking for anything. I never do. I may be a few months younger but I'm more independent and stronger than either of you."

I stamped across the mess of Quinn's room, grabbed the invitation off her desk, and turned around when I got to the door. My sisters looked little and young, their faces peering out from Quinn's closet. "I'll handle this mess myself. I don't need anybody's help. I don't need anybody." I slammed the door behind me.

18

WHILE ANN WOBBLED ONTO the raft, frowning, I held it steady. It was Saturday, eleven in the morning, and I was not digging in dirt with Luke or lounging in the Hamptons with Kirstyn, Gabrielle, and Zhara. I was in my pool coaxing Ann onto a raft. I'd invited her over. Too bad if it was overcast and gray; we were going in the pool. I'd turned the heat way up so we could.

I flipped onto a raft and let myself drift for a few minutes. "You thirsty?"

"No," she said. "You're right though. This is relaxing."

"Mmm-hmm."

"Remember last year when we went, too, to Gabrielle's?"

"Yeah," I said, thinking, *Can't she just not talk about that? I am only barely holding it together as is!*

"I was starving the entire weekend," Ann said.

"Me, too!" I sat up cross-legged on my raft. My mood

had suddenly lifted. "We finally got melon slices for breakfast at like noon?"

"I thought I was going to faint," she said.

"I wake up hungry," I said.

"Me, too." Ann sighed. "Zhara said she wasn't sure she wanted to go but then I guess she decided to."

I lay back down. Ann is great. I've always loved her, her sense of humor, her kind of vulnerable snarkiness. I just wasn't sure I wanted to commit to being me and Ann, the not-as-pretty girls, the not-alpha girls, the girls who'd mope through high school complaining about how bitchy the most popular girls are. Not that I wanted to be bitchy—I just wanted to be happy again, happy and comfortable exactly wherever I was, not looking enviously out of the corners of my eyes.

"Kirstyn's been really, like, hormonal lately," Ann said. "Hasn't she?"

"Yeah."

"To me, anyway," Ann added. "She's been so . . . cold."

"I know."

We floated for a while, then. What neither of us was saying, or would say, in this fragile new alliance, was that if Kirstyn had been cold toward Ann lately, so had I. Before last night, it had been at least a month since I last called her, maybe more. When Kirstyn had said that thing about all of us growing apart lately, the only one it felt true about, for me, was Ann. We had so little left in common. Years ago we liked to imagine stuff together, adventures in her back-yard or mine where we took turns being the tragically dying younger sister (she only has a younger brother) or back in time to prairie days (she'd been obsessed with the *Little House on the Prairie* books by Laura Ingalls Wilder, which I couldn't get through at all; it just seemed like long stretches of weather punctuated by Pa making another chair). Eventually we grew out of that and kind of stuck together by habit and by being in the same group of friends. But over the past few months she'd been a downer and until the funk hit me, too, I wanted to steer clear of it. I didn't want to be dragged down.

So much for that.

But it was kind of, well, relaxing, to be spending the day with her. She wasn't judging my bathing suit or anything else. Mostly she was just agreeing with me.

It was a little awful, how good that felt.

"Anyway," I said up to the gray-white sky, "it's kind of nice to have a break from talking about the graduation party all the time."

"I know it! Don't even get me started on the party! It's like it's really all The Kirstyn Show and we're her syco-phants, paying to bask in her reflected glory."

"We're her what?"

"Sicko-phants? Psycho-fants? I've only read it so I'm not sure how to pronounce it."

"Either way," I said. "I never even read it. But anyway,

exactly. And I for one am sick of being her, whatever, sick elephant."

Ann laughed her burbling belly laugh. "You are so funny, Phoebe."

She flipped over onto her stomach and her raft almost capsized. There was a bobbling moment when she almost went over the right side, overcompensated, dipped in on her left, then, I gotta figure, by supreme willpower, managed to stay on top of the thick blue float. She looked as surprised as I felt at the whole near-crisis, but quickly covered by launching into a whole long story about how Kirstyn was so critical of everything she had chosen from the Crazy Balloon Lady it was not even worth arguing about.

"I finally just started saying okay to whatever she wanted," Ann said. "That's where we were heading anyway. There's just no winning with her, especially when it has to do with 'style.'" Ann started to make quotation marks with her fingers but unbalanced herself slightly and ended up gripping the float instead.

"True," I agreed. Kirstyn had told me about her discussion with Ann, of course, how shockingly tacky the arrangements were that Ann had chosen, how obviously the bargain option. "Too embarrassing," Kirstyn had said, and I agreed. Now, in the pool, I agreed with Ann. Agreement for sale.

"I think Kirstyn only cares that something is the fanciest brand or the most expensive price point," Ann said. "Not actually how it looks. Which is the definition of tacky, if you ask me." Ann started to shrug but almost toppled herself off the raft again. If you just watched Ann you'd think we were shooting the rapids instead of lazing in my pool on a cool windless day.

"True," I said. It was cheering me up, slightly, trashing Kirstyn like this.

"And don't even get me started on the photographer," she started, and her black curly hair bobbled around her pale face. "My mother thinks that is just obscene. A photographer and albums for an eighth-grade graduation party? She's like, *What do these girls think they're planning? A wedding?* She doesn't want to be the one putting on the brakes but she feels like somebody has to. It's out of control."

"You're right," I said. Above me, the clouds were actually breaking apart, revealing a stripe of light blue sky.

"I am?" Ann asked.

"Absolutely." A plan was coming to me, clear as that crack of sky. "I think we have to stop letting ourselves get dragged along like abused puppies. Or psycho elephants, or whatever."

Ann smiled nervously.

"This isn't even really OUR party," I said. "Anymore. As you said."

"True," she said softly. "My mom and I heard some guys talking about it in D'Amico's the other night. High

155

school boys. I swear I never saw these guys before, and they obviously had no idea I even knew about this fabulous party!" Her eyes scanned my face nervously. "But what can we do?"

"We can quit." So easy; it was handed to me on a platter.

"What do you mean, quit?"

"I think you're absolutely right, Ann. This party was supposed to be a celebration of our amazing friendship. The point was us, not trying to be all socialite *Town & Country*. It wasn't supposed to be about only the most fabulous people, the most fabulous centerpieces, the most fabulous dresses . . ."

My voice caught at that. I cleared my throat.

"It was never supposed to be like this," I made myself continue. "But Kirstyn's got her own ideas and we're all supposed to just go along so she can be the center of attention with a bunch of high school boys?"

"You mean those guys from D'Amico's?" Ann asked. "*Kirstyn* told them?"

I shrugged. "You think that was a coincidence? Come on, Ann. Think! That's who she really wants to come. You know, Justin Sachs, all those guys? Which do you think she wants, a graduating-from-eighth-grade party or a look-out-high-school, here-come-the-Pretty-Girls party?"

"Yuck," Ann said.

"Exactly," I agreed.

"And we're all there to, what? Clap for her?"

I smiled. "I guess so." *She's your best friend,* one part of my brain was screaming. *Are you really mocking her and betraying her and selling her out like this? Is this who you want to be?* But another part of my brain screamed back a picture of Kirstyn, twirling under the lights of Gabrielle's fabulous East Hampton patio, surrounded by hot high school boys and laughing about her old friend Phoebe with her middle school bathing suits. Twirling in my green dress.

"Thanks anyway," Ann was saying.

"I just don't think that's how we want to celebrate," I agreed.

We both lay our heads down and let that sink into our skin along with the strengthening sun.

"So we're just, what? Canceling the party?" Ann whispered after a few minutes.

I shrugged without opening my eyes. "I think we have to. Don't you?"

"I already got a dress."

"Ann!"

"I know, you're right, but it's really pretty, mango with ruching, and my mom says it gives me the illusion of a waist."

"Oh, so then maybe we should just go ahead with the party," I said, half sarcastic, half, well, hopeful.

"No, you're right. I just never had the illusion of a waist before. What a waste! Ha!"

"Ha," I tried to agree.

Her smile sank into her rounded chin and she started talking fast. "But like, how will we do it? What will we say? 'Hey, Kirstyn, we decided your whole party is way too tacky so count us out!'" She was practically shouting.

"Something a little subtler, maybe."

"Yeah. How long before it gets all over school?" Ann asked. "Five minutes?"

"Maybe less. By homeroom."

"What do you think everybody will say?"

I shrugged. "Who even knows?" As long as they aren't saying, *Did you hear Phoebe's family lost all their money and can't afford to pay for the party?*

"Kirstyn is going to be furious," Ann whispered.

"She's gonna hate me" slipped out of my mouth.

"Well, you hate her," Ann said. "So you'll be even."

"I do not!" I yelled.

"Just kidding," Ann said, looking away from me.

"I don't!" I started shaking. Why was Ann of all people in my pool? Had I already wrecked everything by saying all this to her? Hate Kirstyn? No way; she's my best friend! But no. This is the best way, I thought. If I didn't cancel for a reason, there'd only be the truth, which would change everything. Not that Kirstyn would dump me or be like *ew, well, if you have no money you're beneath me.* No. It would be so much more subtle. She'd be all like *poor you, you're poor!* And she might be nice about it but she would pull away soon, I know she would, as if it were contagious. She's

158

already been pulling away from me, for nothing—but if she knew this, oh, she'd be sweet and generous, sad-eyed, pausing on her way down the hall linked-arms with Gabrielle to ask me, her poor charity case, if everything was okay. No! I think I saw a movie once when I was home sick in like third grade about a rich girl whose father died and then the fancy boarding school where she went found out she was poor and she had to dress in rags and be taunted by all her old friends—holy crap, that movie totally haunted my nightmares when I was younger and I had completely forgotten about it until this very second! No way was I turning into that poor taunted girl!

"I don't hate her," I told Ann more calmly, though as I was saying it, the image of Kirstyn twirling around in my green dress overwhelmed me. "It just really feels, to me anyway, like canceling the party is the right thing to do."

She sighed nervously. "You don't think they'll just go ahead and have it without us?"

"No!" Yikes. Everybody would think they kicked us out. "No way."

"Yeah," Ann sighed. "Zhara might actually be relieved if it's cancelled."

I tried not to sound as desperate as I felt. "Has she said anything?"

"You know Zhara. She would never say a bad word about anybody."

"Unlike us."

159

"Yeah. Unlike anybody," Ann said.

Why wasn't I best friends with Zhara? I got the feeling at the beginning of this year that she wanted to be, but I held back. Stupid, stupid. She would never say anything bad about anybody. I probably even could have told her about Mom. Poop on a stick.

"But I can sense Zhara sort of feels like the party is out of control, a little, too."

"So maybe she would agree with us," I said, sounding pathetic. "And Gabrielle? I just don't see her caring that much about the party, any of the details . . . She's kind of, like, above it. Not in a snobby way, but, you know?"

"Yeah," Ann said. "Totally. That's why I think Kirstyn sticks to her like a barnacle—she's terrified of being demoted to the second social rung next year, if Gabrielle ditches her. It used to be you for a while; now it's Gabrielle."

It used to be me? *Used to be?*

Ann shrugged. "Kirstyn's got an alpha-girl magnet."

"It's sad, really," I finally managed to say, meaning: everything.

"It is," Ann said. "It really is."

I nodded. Kirstyn really had tried to make the party so elaborate and exclusive, to be the one true boss of us all, so desperate to be next to the alpha girl. So shallow! I suddenly couldn't believe what a spoiled brat she was, or that I'd never let myself admit it.

"Well," I said. "We have to stand up for ourselves. We can't keep letting ourselves get pushed around, right?"

"I guess not," Ann said, tilting her head sideways, quizzically.

"No, we're not. You know why?"

"Why?"

I jumped off my raft into the pool. The warm water came up to my waist. "Because nobody, nothing can intimidate us. We will never back down, we will never surrender. Especially not to moody, needy girls. We are warrior women!" I yelled, grabbing her raft. "We are Valkyries! We will not—ever—allow ourselves to be bullied or mistreated! Right?"

Ann tumbled off the raft into the pool. When she came up, she pushed her hair out of her eyes and dabbed at her smeared mascara. "We're what?"

"We're strong enough to stand up to her." Her dunking had kind of ruined the flow of my rousing speech. It wasn't her fault; I had startled her and maybe actually jostled her raft in my enthusiasm, but still I couldn't help feeling slightly annoyed.

"I hope so." Ann shuddered a little, then said, "Well, my mother will be happy, at least."

"Oh, please," I said, shivering a bit myself. "I think we'll all be happy. Except, maybe, Kirstyn."

19

SUNDAY MORNING, ACTUALLY afternoon, my father sat beside me on my bed. No matter how many times I pulled the covers over my head and cocooned inside there, he continued to tug them down again, telling me I had to get up.

I opened one eye and squinted at him. He had pulled back the curtains so my room was flooded with light. I groaned, trying to pull the covers up over me again but then he got a better grip on them than I had and he wouldn't let me.

I told him I was sick, I told him to leave me alone, I told him this was a vacation weekend memorializing something so I deserved to be left alone to sleep in during it. He didn't answer but he didn't budge either, and didn't ease his grip on my covers. I decided boring him to death would have to do, and consciously relaxed my face, eyes closed, resolved to outwait him. I didn't want to wake up. Sleeping through the rest of the weekend was my best escape from thoughts of Tuesday morning.

Just when I thought maybe he had left and it was a phantom feeling, not really him depressing the side of my bed, he said, "Kirstyn's mother left a message on Mom's voice mail."

My eyes were still closed and I concentrated on not moving any muscles, as I thought, fast, what that meant. Must be about the bounced check, which means he now knows I haven't said anything to my friends yet about getting out of the party. Either Mom called Kirstyn's mom back or Daddy did or neither of them did yet and I still had time to stop them from making the call.

"About what?" I asked, fake-sleepily.

"She said she wanted to talk about the graduation party."

"Did Mom call her back?"

"Not yet," he said, shifting slightly.

Phew. "We're canceling it," I said.

He didn't say anything.

I opened my eyes and sat up. "When Ann was over yesterday, we had a long talk about it and it turns out we just both felt like the party was out of control, anyway. She's been really uncomfortable for a while about doing such an over-the-top expensive, elaborate party, and I think she was relieved that I felt the same way. You were right. It was too much. I think really everybody was feeling that and just needed someone to be like, you know what? We don't have to do this!" I smiled manically at Daddy, who was looking at me very seriously. "So we cancelled the party. So, that's all good, now."

Daddy nodded a couple of times slowly. He didn't ask how the rest of the girls reacted or even if I had actually said anything to them yet.

"So tell Mom not to bother calling Kirstyn's mother back, because, well, there's no party to talk about!" I tried to calm down because I was starting to scare myself. "Okay? I mean, Mom has enough to worry about, right?"

"Okay," he said simply, and patted my leg through the blanket.

"Great, thanks, Daddy."

"You're a good person, Phoebe."

"Yeah. I'm awesome." In the past when things all fell into place so easily for me, it made me happy. I flopped back down and pulled the covers over my head. He had lost his grip on them in his misplaced moment of paternal pride.

"It's a beautiful day. You should be outside playing."

"Oh, please! Playing outside? How old do you think I am, six?"

"I'll make you a deal." He grabbed the blanket and yanked it off my bed.

"What?" I curled up, all exposed.

"I will let you laze around all day today," he offered, "do whatever you want, but tomorrow you come fishing with me."

"Ugh," I said, although it actually sounded kind of nice. It had been years since I'd gone on one of his Memorial Day fishing trips. He and a bunch of his friends would all go out on their buddy Fonso Lombardi's boat, chasing bluefish. They'd get up when it was still dark out, load up their cars with beer, soda, and junk food, and by dawn they'd already be out on Long Island Sound, shivering against the cold, mocking one another mercilessly and digging into the coolers, and occasionally fishing. A few years ago they got the idea it would be fun to bring their kids. Both my sisters and most of the other kids hated it, probably because they spent so much of the day throwing up over the sides of the boat. My sisters groaned from then on anytime Daddy mentioned fishing so I did, too. I had actually loved the whole day, but I wasn't about to admit it. Last year he hadn't even mentioned bringing us.

"Deal or no deal?" he asked, my blanket in his hand.

"Deal," I said, groaning, as if it were the day in bed I wanted and not the next morning trudging out of my father's car at the docks, bundled in fleeces and the comfortable quiet, then rocking in the rhythmic waves eating doughnuts at dawn. I tried to frown away my smile.

"Okay, then," Daddy said, tucking me back in. "I'm glad it worked out with the party, sweetheart. Well done."

That got rid of my smile, fast.

I stayed in bed most of the day, getting up only to go to the bathroom and, later, to eat some bean soup Gosia had made and left in the fridge. Nobody was around; the house was quiet. I went back upstairs, wrote my graduation speech—comparing our graduation class to soup, since my English teacher is totally into metaphors and soup was on my mind—and then fell hard asleep. I guess I really was tired. When my father woke me up, I thought it was midnight.

"No, sweetheart," he whispered. "It's almost five. Time to go."

I blinked my eyes in the darkness but nothing was distinguishable from anything else.

"Phoebe," he said, a warning in his voice, but he didn't have to worry; I was wide awake and felt better than I had in weeks.

"I'm up," I said. "Be ready in five minutes."

"That's my girl," he whispered, and kissed my forehead. When he closed my door, I bolted out of bed. In four minutes I was down in the kitchen, green and white swimsuit (who cares?) under layers of T-shirts and fleeces, a ponytail in my dirty hair, gulping down a big glass of orange juice. My father was bent over, zipping up the smaller of our two huge coolers. He winked at me and we headed out to the garage.

The thought crossed my mind in the damp dark that I was lucky I hadn't gone to the Hamptons with Gabrielle, Kirstyn, and Zhara, but I pushed that thought away as I helped load the bigger cooler into the trunk. They weren't going to intrude on my day, not even in the negative. And it was not just the slight possibility Luke would be there with his father that had made me grab my lip gloss. I just didn't want to get chapped lips. Seriously, wind, cold sea air . . . Even though he'd specifically said he was working with his mom Saturday, not Monday, Luke probably wouldn't be on the boat anyway, which was just fine with me.

Closing my eyes in the shotgun seat beside my father as we made our slow way down toward the shore, following the beams of our headlights, I felt confident that what lay ahead of me was a perfect stretch of hours, a gift of a day that had nothing to do with anything in my life, a break. I would fish and stuff my face with doughnuts, maybe get to steer the boat, work on my tan, maybe even catch a big ugly bluefish if I got really lucky. The possibility of being lucky felt real to me again, and I resolved to keep it, to breathe in the good salty smell of no worries, to hoard all the sweetness of this day before the end of all my friendships, to keep the whole day free of anything but easy.

But, no.

20

NEITHER OF US SAID HELLO. I pretended not to see him. I'm not sure if he was pretending or just actually not seeing me. It was so early, and still dark, and really cold. I bent down to tie my already-tied sneaker as he and his father passed us.

"Hey, Paul," my father said to his father. "Hey, Luke."

I glanced up and caught their hands lowering from having waved in response. *I can manage this,* I told myself, grabbing the smaller cooler. *No big deal if Luke is here, too.* I took a deep breath of the salty air for courage and crunched across the gravel toward the boats.

I shivered, stepping onto the boat behind my father, taking his hand.

"Cold?" he asked.

I shook my head. The good thing about men is they seem to feel no need to chat with one another. None of them even smiled. They all sort of grunted, at most, and settled into spots, their thermal cups of coffee (or in Daddy's case, tea) gripped in their hands, their caps pulled low over their eyebrows.

I was the only girl, the only female on the trip, and the only kid other than Luke. Fonso Lombardi clapped me on the back and told me he was glad to have me aboard again.

"You're not planning to puke this time, are you?"

"Nope," I said, and added softly because I couldn't not, "I didn't last time, either."

I don't think he heard me; he was already onto his next back-clap: Luke. "You know Luke, right? Phoebe, Luke. You're about the same age, right?"

I nodded.

"Good, good," Fonso said, releasing our backs. He lifted his *captain* hat just long enough to swipe the meaty palm of his other hand across his big bald head. I tensed for his next questions, but thankfully he went to do something with ropes along with his first mate. Fonso is a great guy, I've always liked him and Luke's dad best of Daddy's friends, but still an adult is an adult and can therefore be counted on to make you feel like an absolute dork at the worst possible moment.

Luke hadn't even nodded. He could've nodded.

My father and Luke's sat beside each other in the stern of the boat. Luke and I each sat on the other sides of our fathers. I spread my knees and steadied myself for the slow trip through the marina. My father passed me his cup, offering to share his tea. I shook my head. Three years ago, when he forced Quinn and Allison to come, too, the three of us chattered the whole way out, having a great time, trying to cheer up all the glum-looking guys. Daddy's friends teased him, later in the day, for living in a harem. By then my sisters were worn out and seasick, and Daddy threw his arm around me and took me up front and stood beside me while Fonso let me take the wheel. This time I wasn't going to chatter. I pulled my cap lower, tightened my ponytail through the back hole, and looked out past the masts of the tethered sailboats, toward open water.

An hour later, when the sky had turned white but the water was still black, the thrumming of the engine stopped. Its echo lingered in my ears as the mate brought out the gear for us all. He asked me if I knew how to work it and I told him yes, but nothing more. I hoped I remembered. I wasn't about to be the one incompetent on board.

Each of us took a position and dropped our hooks into the water.

"Ten bucks apiece in the pot? First guy who catches something wins half, biggest fish gets the other," Fonso announced, patting his huge, perfectly round belly. He glanced at me. "Or girl."

I nodded at him. All the guys muttered agreement.

Fonso peered into the water as if he could assess the position of his hook in there. "I'm feeling lucky today," he said, his deep voice echoing off the water. He reached into his huge cooler and pulled out a can of beer. The pop of the top was followed by a happy little fizzle. "Who else?"

"I'm always feeling lucky," my dad said, turning around. "Lucky is just being on the boat."

Fonso held the opened beer can toward Daddy.

"Oh. No thanks," Daddy said. "No beer before breakfast for me."

"So eat a doughnut first," Fonso suggested.

Luke's father laughed. "Breakfast of champions," he said, reeling in his line, checking his empty hook, and letting it back out again. Luke's father, like Luke, is solid and strong, with tan-looking skin all year and dark hair, though Luke's is a little wavier. But I wasn't looking at Luke, and I certainly wasn't thinking about him, either. I reeled in my hook and let it out again, reeled and lowered, thanking whatever powers exist for the chance to just do something mechanical all day long and not have to explain or be cool or witty.

It's Luke's fault I turned around. I heard him laugh, or I thought it was him, and it messed up my rhythm. I just turned for a second to see what was so funny that he would kind of hiccup-laugh. I had been completely minding my own business before that moment, not thinking about the fact that he was directly behind me and ignoring me because probably he hated me and I had blown my last chance to get back together with him, for nothing. I was not even thinking how cute he looked in that old faded blue-gray sweatshirt that had clearly been his father's because the cuffs were turned up a few times, and the washed-out green baseball cap with his dark hair curling a little bit around at the edges. No, not me, I was just fishing. But then he went and messed me up with that noise of his, or whoever's, which might have been the clearing of a throat of the *excuse me* type, in which case it would have been rude to ignore it.

I am just not a rude person.

So I turned around, which would have been fine and maybe nobody even would have caught my quick little glance behind me to see if someone was ahem-ing at me or not, if I hadn't had my fishing rod in my hand at the time. With its hook out of the water.

The hook was the actual problem, because it kind of got ahead of me and swung across the deck of the boat. I don't even think I swung it; a breeze probably picked it up and whipped it across. From the way those guys reacted you'd have thought I suddenly pulled a rifle out from under my sweatshirt or something. Fonso grabbed the rod away from me, but by then it was too late.

The hook was in Luke's arm.

He didn't bleed all that much, since luckily he still had his sweatshirt on; the barbed point of the hook barely lodged in the skin just above his left wrist. His father was able to work it out in a second, maybe two. Luke looked pale but didn't cry or scream like I probably would've. The

mate brought over a first-aid kit and did a whole number with an alcohol wipe and a butterfly Band-Aid. Luke's father kept trying to convince Luke to sit down for a minute but he was like, *no, I'm fine, I'm fine.*

Daddy whispered loud in my ear, "Say you're sorry."

I scowled at him and whispered, "It was an accident."

He gave me a look like, *duh, I didn't think you were trying to wound the guy.* How little he knows.

"Sorry," I said to Luke.

"Forget it," Luke said, already leaning over the other side of the boat, away from me.

"Lucky Phoebe," Fonso said. "She wins! First catch of the day!"

Everybody gave him a little chuckle and went back to fishing. As grateful as I was to good old Fonso, I could only keep reeling in and out for another few minutes after that, and not just because he and my father were not being as subtle as they thought they were at keeping an eye on me.

"Gonna take a break," I said. Daddy and Fonso were all over my rod and reel before I got the words out, securing my hook. "Hungry," I explained.

"Sure, sweetheart," Daddy said encouragingly. "Why don't you open those muffins and doughnuts we brought?"

I sat down on the seat and shoved a muffin in my mouth in almost one bite. The paper was off the second one before I swallowed the first. I love lemon poppy seed muffins and even the ruination of this last good day

seemed unable to dampen my morning hunger pangs.

I stared at the backs of all the guys and wondered what in the world ever possessed me to make me think this would be a fun thing to commit to, a full day trapped with no possibility of escape. I chugged a full can of seltzer and when my eyes ran from the bubbles it felt good.

It started to drizzle around seven.

I went below deck to go to the bathroom and for a change of scenery from the thick gray up top. While washing my hands, I bared my teeth at myself in the mirror, Kirstyn's habit. Oh, no. A poppy seed was trapped right between my two front teeth.

Great. I tried to dig it out with my pinky fingernail but only managed to wedge it in farther. No dental floss under the sink or in any cabinets in the kitchen, no toothpicks. I was starting to draw blood from my gums but that little black dot was cemented in there tight. Great. Stuck on a boat with the boy I love who hates me for a full day with a frigging poppy seed in my teeth.

Fine, so? I wasn't planning to smile anyway.

In desperation I grabbed the only thing I could find, a corkscrew, and tried to brace myself against the rolling rhythm of the boat to work on the demented cemented poppy seed, using the mirror behind the downstairs bar, when Luke showed up.

"What are you doing?" he asked, as if he'd caught me torturing a puppy.

174

"Nothing!" I hid the corkscrew behind my back. Very mature, I know.

"Okay." He turned away.

"Luke," I said, careful to keep my lips over my teeth. Luckily his name is Luke, which makes you kind of pucker, and not Ezekiel.

"What?" He turned slowly back toward me.

"Sorry," I said.

"Doesn't even hurt," he said, turning away again.

"I didn't mean the hook," I said. "I mean, about everything. This weekend."

He shrugged without looking back. "Whatever." He went into the little bathroom and closed the door. I had maybe a minute to get the poppy seed out and think of something brilliant to say to him. Did he really mean whatever? That's the exact thing he said after that day in seventh grade, when I . . .

When I did exactly what I did this time to him. Ugh. The problem was, I had gone away to camp the morning after Luke and I had our first-ever private kiss, in the back hall of my house, when he had come over to give me a going-to-camp-present of a box of stationery with a matching pen. As I was opening the wrapping paper, his dad and mine had wandered into the kitchen together and when I looked up at Luke to thank him for the gift, which was really cute though a little girlier than something I would normally buy, pink and purple stripes with hearts and flowers around the edges, he was blushing and staring at his feet. "I hope you like it," he mumbled.

"I do," I said, and without really thinking, I had leaned toward him, to kiss him thank-you the way I kiss like my aunt Tillie when she gives me a gift. But Luke is not my aunt Tillie. I had been aiming for his cheek, but he turned his face and met my lips with his own.

Our fathers were a few feet away; only a wall and an open door separated us from them. When I opened my eyes and then Luke opened his, we pulled back, but then just stood there staring softly at each other until our fathers came out talking loudly about the Yankees. Luke's dad asked if he was ready to go. He whispered bye to me and left for the summer.

His family was invited over to our house for a barbecue on August 30. Allison put mascara on me. "He hasn't seen you in more than two months," she told me. "You have to look good." But he hadn't come. Just his parents did. They said he wasn't feeling well, and apologized, but if he had been really sick, would they be out having fun at our house? I spent most of that night sulking in front of the TV, talking to Kirstyn on the phone. Allison brought up a pint of Rocky Road in solidarity.

So the first day of seventh grade I ignored him. The second day I was waiting for my friends on the upper field when Luke walked right up to me and said hello. Before I could answer, Kirstyn, Gabrielle, Ann, and Zhara were suddenly there, all around me.

"What are you *doing*?" Kirstyn asked me.

"Nothing," I answered nervously, almost honestly.

"You don't still like Luke, do you?" she demanded, as if it were laughable, almost ridiculous to ask such a thing.

What could I say? Saying yes was clearly the wrong answer, and was I really supposed to go way out on that limb? When he hadn't even come over? When he had pretty much said, with actions if not words, that he didn't like me anymore?

"Of course not!" I said, and Kirstyn, laughing with our friends and with me, led me away from Luke, who looked like he'd been punched in the gut. I never found out if he still liked me. I think he might've, and I know I still liked him. But I ran away laughing with my friends anyway. I know Kirstyn was totally trying to help me, keep me from making a fool of myself, but it felt wrong anyway.

And now I'd blown him off for my friends again. Well, and then impaled him with a fish hook. No wonder he hated me. I'd hate me if I were him. I was pretty close to hating me as it was and I'm me!

I heard the toilet flush inside the boat's tiny bathroom and the water go on in the sink. I had maybe ten seconds. The poppy seed was vying for permanent residence between my teeth. The door swung out on its hinges.

"Luke," I said, sucking my sore teeth and spinning to face him.

He looked at me coolly.

"I know you probably hate me," I said. "But . . ."

He raised his eyebrows, waiting.

A choice, again. Be safe and cool, or tell the truth?

"But I still like you," I said, and turned my back to him this time.

I waited for something to happen. All my senses were on alert: I could smell the salty water splashing on the sides of the boat, hear all the voices up above, feel the moisture in the air touching my skin. He hadn't budged or made a sound. He could say it was too late, he could come to me and touch my arms with his hands. I heard a footstep, and then another. Just as I was giving myself permission to hope, I heard his foot hit the step. Up he went, up and up, away from me.

So that was that. After a few minutes mangling myself with the corkscrew without success, I hauled myself up the steps into the damp chill of the deck and took up my position again. There was nothing to do but fish, so I fished. Fonso moved the boat a couple of times before we landed I guess in the middle of a school of blues. We started hoisting them in one after another. I hooked a monster and reeled him in slow, letting him have some slack to tire himself out, then pulling him in again. When I finally got him, Fonso netted him and dumped him onto the deck and I shocked us all, wanting to pull the hook out myself. I won for biggest fish of the day, as well as first catch (with an asterisk for it having been a boy rather than a fish), and on the way back in, I leaned against my father, feeling nothing more than smelly, damp, and tired. The wadded up $110 I'd won was zipped into the pocket of my fleece. Luke still hadn't talked to me but at that moment I was willing to let go of it and just watch the wake spread out behind us.

After we docked, I was collecting my bag of filleted fish from the mate and, turning around, smacked into Luke. "Sorry," I said.

"Hey," he said.

I stopped.

"I don't," he said.

I felt myself deflate. But what did I expect? And why did he have to rub it in? He had made himself clear already with his silence.

"Whatever," I said back.

"Wait," he said, catching up to me on the dock where I was following my father.

"What? I got it. Okay already. You don't like me. I don't blame you."

"No. I mean, I don't . . . hate you," Luke said.

I stopped. He was right behind me. My father kept walking, oblivious. I didn't want to turn around, and not just because I had my hands full of fish and my teeth full of poppy seed.

"At all," he whispered, his voice so close to my ear I could feel the breath that carried the words.

I swallowed. "Okay."

"Okay," he said, too.

Then I started walking again, and didn't look back, even after I was in the car, heading toward home. He didn't hate me. Not at all.

"You look happy," Daddy said as we pulled up the driveway.

"I am," I admitted.

"Me, too," he said.

Luke doesn't hate me, I stopped myself from explaining. Not *at all*.

Daddy cooked up the bluefish for dinner and everybody went nuts over how delicious it was. That's all Mom and Dad and Quinn and Allison talked about, rather than everything that was actually happening. Any time there was a silence that threatened to let another topic slip in, one of them would combine the words *bluefish* and *delicious* in a slightly new variation. I hardly tasted it, myself. After all that wind on the boat all day, I could still feel the echo of Luke's exhale across my left cheek.

21

TUESDAY MORNING, JUST AS the sky started pinking up, I tip-toed down to the kitchen and slid the $110 I had won into the emergency envelope. If it had been ten or twenty times that amount, I might have been tempted to keep it myself and use it to fund the party. Before all this happened, I would've just spent it on nothing. It was mine, after all. But it might help somebody in an emergency. That almost empty envelope kept bothering my mind; it felt better to have it filled. And maybe, even, to be the one filling it. I closed the drawer feeling a tiny bit better.

When I heard the new tea kettle already nearing a boil, though, I sprinted back up the stairs and crouched in the upstairs den until my heart stopped pounding. Then I went up to Gosia's room and waited. When she came out I asked her to drive me to school. She looked at me sadly. I told her I had a really important early meeting before school for a project, which was kind of close to the truth.

She said no problem, go get dressed.

I was taking my chances toasting a waffle when I heard footsteps behind me. Thinking, *Thank goodness Gosia is fast,* I said, "Great, I'm ready, just incinerating a waffle and I'll eat it in the car."

"Sounds delicious," she said, only it wasn't Gosia, it was Mom.

I spun around. "Oh," I said.

Behind me the button popped up again. I spun back around, thankful for the distraction. Mom was in her suit already, briefcase in hand, beautiful as ever. The waffle, on the other hand, was still pale and sagging under the weight of its barely melting ice crystals. I opened the door and pulled it out. It crunched when I bit into it, still being solidly frozen beyond the limp damp outer edges. Not gourmet, but I wasn't about to be forced to eat coal this morning. This morning was already going to be lousy enough.

Coming into the kitchen behind Mom, Gosia jiggled her keys and asked, "Ready?"

"Yeah." I grabbed my bag with my other hand and rushed toward the back door. Allison was coming down the stairs, with Quinn right behind her. "I have an early meeting!" I said frantically, grabbing my flip-flops from the floor between them.

Allison raised one eyebrow.

"Me, too," Mom said, head bent over her BlackBerry.

"With the lawyer?" Quinn asked her, pushing past me, but I didn't wait to hear an answer. Instead I followed Gosia out to the car.

Gosia didn't turn on her music as we drove and thankfully didn't talk to me either. The day was gray and chilly and I sank down in my seat, not wanting to watch it go by out the window. At the red light just before school, Gosia held out her pack of gum to me. I took a piece as the light turned green.

"Tough day ahead?" she asked.

I nodded.

"Those are Allison's flip-flops."

I looked down. "Yeah."

"Good luck," Gosia whispered, slowing to a stop.

"Thanks." I got out of the car in the deserted circle. After the taillights were gone around the corner, I stopped pretending to rush inside; I let go of the door handle at the front of school and went over to sit down against the brick wall near where the buses drop off. Waiting, I tucked my hands up into my jean jacket sleeves. Despite the gray of the morning, I slipped my sunglasses on. I needed to hide behind them, even if there was no sun. It was hard to believe it had been so hot I'd been sweating, swimming, when? Last week? Though not as hard to believe as the fact that I was sitting there thinking about the weather instead of what to say to Kirstyn, whose bus was pulling into the circle at that very second.

Where was Ann? No way was I doing this myself. How totally unfair!

Kirstyn got off our bus in front of Luke and William, who were deep in conversation, laughing together. They didn't even glance my way. Kirstyn saw me immediately and ran right over. "Hey," she said. "I thought you were sick or something. Why weren't you on the bus?"

Before I could concoct an answer, Gabrielle, getting off the next bus, yelled, "Kirstyn! Phoebe!"

Luke had his back to me, talking to William, Dean, and a few other guys. Like he didn't even notice me. Like nothing had happened, nothing was going on between us, he was just joking around with his buddies. Well, nothing actually was going on, nothing official. What had I expected? I had other stuff to deal with anyway so it was just as well that he hadn't come over to say hello or *how was the bluefish* or *will you go out with me* or *can you believe this weather.*

"Good weekend?" I asked Kirstyn as Gabrielle made her way toward us. My voice had none of the casual lightness I'd been trying for.

Kirstyn tried to look into my eyes but luckily my sunglasses were a shield. "Not as good as it would've been if you'd been there," she said. Smiling, she turned to Gabrielle. "Right?"

"Oh, definitely," Gabrielle agreed. "We kept saying something is missing—oh, wait, I know! Phoebe!"

Gabrielle and Kirstyn laughed together at the memory of that hilarious comment. "Seriously. I made my parents promise next time I won't get shafted like that, so unfair. My brother had four friends there. Why couldn't I? We brought you and Ann these."

She held out two yarn bracelets, one pink and red, one yellow and green. I chose the pink and red and Kirstyn was tying it around my wrist when I noticed, first, that she and Gabrielle had yarn bracelets on, too, and second that Ann and Zhara's bus was disgorging its passengers. Zhara looked more relaxed than ever, her dark hair down in back and the front just held back by a tiny clip. She was wearing a navy and turquoise yarn bracelet and, I noticed as she came closer, slightly sparkly gloss on her dark lips.

Ann, on the other hand, looked like a nervous wreck, her hair standing practically straight up, her face blotchy and puffy, brown eyeliner smudged under her left eye like a bruise.

Kirstyn and Gabrielle were immediately cooing over how pretty Zhara looked, asking if her mother liked her makeover. As Ann chewed on her lower lip, Gabrielle said, "Oh, Ann, we brought you this!" and handed her the bracelet. Ann's eyes, full of alarm, flicked up to mine. I shrugged; she let Kirstyn tie it on her.

The warning bell was ringing. I had six minutes to do this. *Oh, dread.* I stood up and glanced at Ann, which was a mistake; she interpreted it as a push to start, and she said, of all things, "Wait. Don't go in yet. Phoebe and I have something to say."

We all stared at Ann. Her neck was red and her face was bluish white. She looked dangerously ill. "You okay?" Zhara asked her, putting her hand on Ann's shoulder.

Ann nodded, pleading with me with her eyes, which made everybody turn and look, horrifyingly, at me.

I tried to smile. "It's nothing, it's just . . ." *Here we go. Do it.* "We were talking about the party."

"Oh, so were we!" Gabrielle answered, her huge smile lighting up the day. "We couldn't stop talking about it, or at least Kirstyn couldn't. I think she may even have roped one of my cousins into coming, and Miles said he'd definitely be there unless he has regionals that night."

I closed my eyes behind my glasses.

"What?" Gabrielle asked.

Ann was clearly not going to be any help. She was barely breathing, leaning against the wall.

"It's just . . . it's starting to feel a little out of control," I mumbled.

"Are you kidding?" Gabrielle asked. "It's totally out of control! The invitations aren't going out until today and everybody's already booked hair appointments! Did you hear what those girls—"

"I mean," I interrupted, "it's starting to feel like, stupid. Too big, too much, nothing to do with us, really, I mean the five of us, and everybody in our grade and . . . It's just like, I don't know."

"What's wrong, Phoebe?" Zhara asked, looking concerned.

Kirstyn tilted her head at me and said softly, "It's going to be great, Phoebe, don't worry. It's going to be the best night of our lives so far, just like you promised." She put her arm around me, like comforting me, and that was more than I could take. I shook her off.

"No, Kirstyn," I said. "It's not. Forget it. It's not OUR party anymore, it's yours. It's all about you, your taste, what you want, your flower arrangements, your stupid little photo albums, your perfect shoes not dyed to match. It was supposed to be about our friendship, not about you in the green dress, the center of attention as always."

Her mouth dropped open.

"Phoebe," Gabrielle said. "I can't believe you would say that."

I clenched my jaw, thinking, *Sure, you're Kirstyn's new best friend, you should defend her, Gabrielle. Just watch out when she finds somebody new and drops you, too.*

"If you want the green dress, you can have it," Kirstyn said.

"It is totally not about the green dress," I shrieked, louder than I'd intended. I tried to settle my voice, my breathing, my heart. "It's just . . . tacky, the whole overblown party. My parents think it's disgusting, and honestly so do my sisters, and so do I. And so does Ann."

"You do?" Zhara asked Ann.

"I guess," Ann said meekly.

"She does," I said. "We just feel like it's ridiculous and gross and honestly I don't want to be a part of something that reeks of *ooh, look how great and rich and pretty we are!*"

Now it was not just my small circle of friends staring at me, it was everybody on their way into school. Even Bridget Burgess stopped, her hands in the pockets of the jeans that used to be Quinn's, and watched as if this were a show being put on for her benefit.

Luke turned around. When he saw me, he smiled a little. "How was the bluefish?" he asked.

"Um, good," I answered.

"She caught like a thirty pounder," he said to my friends, who nodded a little numbly.

"We're kind of in the middle of a big fight here," Gabrielle told him.

"Yeah, I gathered," Luke said as the bell rang. "Well, you going in?" he asked me.

"Um, soon," I said.

"Flirt much?" Kirstyn asked coldly.

"No," I said, not looking at Luke.

"Why don't you just admit you like him already, Phoebe?"

I glared at her. Forget it. I wasn't giving in anymore, I was just sick of it. Too bad. "I did," I said. "I do. I like him. I admit it."

"It's about time," Kirstyn said.

"Yeah," Luke said, behind me.

"I just think it's so lame when a person feels like she has to hide the truth from her best friends," Kirstyn said. "It's so . . . insulting."

"It's not about *you*, Kirstyn," I said. "Believe it or not, not everything is about you!"

"I never said it was," she snapped back. "I was talking about *you!*"

"Well, we'll be late . . ." Luke said. He waited a second but we weren't budging, obviously, so he and his buddies headed in.

Kirstyn and I had turned away from each other. I could see Gabrielle looking back and forth between us but I wasn't backing down this time.

"Come on, you guys," Gabrielle whispered. "Let's just forget this happened and go in. By lunchtime we'll . . ."

"No, Gabrielle," I said. "We can't just move on, and not everything is fine. Kirstyn said it herself—'*I think it's clear to all of us that this is good-bye.*' Remember? Well, I for one just don't see any reason to have my good-byes catered and photographed."

"You're not . . ." Zhara started. "You don't want to do the party?"

I glared at her.

She swallowed hard. "So wait, just the four of us, then, or, Ann, are you pulling out, too?"

"I guess," Ann said.

Zhara put her hand on her hip. "How can we . . ."

"We can't," Kirstyn said, flipping her sunglasses down onto her face. "We'll just cancel."

"But what about the deposit?" Zhara asked.

"My mother will take care of it, don't worry," Kirstyn said. "It will be worth it to me, to be done with this whole thing. I never wanted to do the stupid party in the first place."

"That's not what you were saying this weekend," Gabrielle objected.

"Shut up, Gabrielle," Kirstyn said. "Phoebe is right. It's over." She turned and stormed toward school, leaving the rest of us, as always, to straggle in after her.

190

22

I WON, I TOLD MYSELF. I did it. *And it went surprisingly smoothly, too.*

So why did I feel so bad?

I ambled through my classes, doodling in my now-useless party planning speckled notebook, with the purple Sharpie Kirstyn had bought in the five-pack, to give us each one. Everything was connected to her. We did our best not to look at each other. Well, actually everybody was doing their best to stay out of my way. I went to the library at lunch and opened my party planning notebook and began a list:

REASONS I AM LUCKY TO BE
OUT OF THE PARTY

1. No other choice—had to get out of it
2. You can't choose friends over family
3. Green dress

Then I cried for a minute, hiding behind the math text-book I was pretending to study. I tore out that page and started a new list on the next:

WHY I HATE MYSELF
1. *I just wrecked my friendship with my best friend.*
2. *Maybe she's selfish and materialistic, but she's been my best friend for four years.*
3. *I'm not going to have a graduation party.*
4. *Nobody likes me anymore.*
5. *I am in the library at lunch.*
6. *The way Kirstyn looked at me just before she went in to school.*
7. *The way she hasn't looked at me since.*
8. *I am probably going to have to sit in the high school library every lunch period for the next four years.*
9. *Kirstyn will never forgive me and neither will any of my other friends, ex-friends I mean, because I have no friends now.*

I sat there reading over my list for a while. It was really bad. But the main reason wasn't on it. As the end-of-lunch bell rang, I added a final reason to hate myself:

10. *As much bad stuff as I can (and did) say about Kirstyn, she is not the real reason I canceled the party, and I blamed her anyway.*

I collected my books and left the library. All afternoon I tried to convince myself that it didn't really matter. What I had said was all true. It was ridiculous to spend so much money, or make our parents spend it, for an eighth-grade graduation party. Kirstyn does like to be the center of attention. She does want to exclude people, and she does look down on you if your family is not in the same league as hers. Even if I had told her the truth, it would have ended our friendship anyway, probably. The Phoebe she liked was happy, smooth, easy, untroubled. But that's not me anymore. So what does it matter, ultimately, if I blamed her? She is at fault on some level. Isn't she?

I didn't go to track, even though our last meet of the year was coming up in two days and if you miss a practice you don't run. I didn't care. No way could I have run anyway. I could barely drag myself up to the speed of sulk. I sank down in the back row of the early bus and kept my eyes closed the whole way home.

Mom was sitting on the front steps when I got there, talking on her cell phone and fiddling absently with her necklace, the sapphire on the thin silver chain. She hung up as I got to the walk. She was wearing thick socks, jeans, and a pale pink long-sleeve T-shirt.

I stopped in front of her. Maybe she wanted to be alone. She looked kind of like a kid, her arms resting on her knees like that. I wondered for the first time in my life if it might be better to have a mom who was big and chubby and could gather me in her arms and rock me.

"Hi," I said.

"Hi," she said.

I swallowed. "Well . . . I guess I'll go in and . . ."

"Wait."

I stopped. *Oh, dread.* I sat down a few feet from her on the front step and looked at the front yard, out to our hedges that were still only medium.

She sighed, kind of sadly.

I should never come home early, I thought. *What if she started to cry? I wouldn't know how to deal with that at all. She's the mom. The grown-up. She's not supposed to fall apart, especially not in front of me. I can't handle it!*

My hand levitated again and hovered near her shoulder and then, almost maybe by accident, landed on it. I felt her boney shoulder tense under my fingers and I almost pulled away, scalded, but then, I didn't.

Her shoulder relaxed.

I slipped my hand around to her other shoulder and pulled her toward me. She came easily and rested her head against my shoulder. Neither of us said anything more. We just sat there like that and I looked out at the tulips blooming down by the hedges, which I had never noticed before. It was nice, kind of. It felt good. It was weirdly comforting, to comfort her.

"You know what's so dumb?" she asked, pulling away.

Me? "What?" I was a little disappointed but also a little

relieved because my arm was starting to fall asleep. It's not in shape for that, I guess.

"Double doors." She pointed behind us to the massive entrance we never use.

"That's what's dumb?"

"I was so freakishly proud of these double doors. The day we bought the house, while you girls were in school, Daddy and I came over after we signed the contracts and I threw these double doors open and stood in the wide space there, surveying all the grandeur I had just bought for my family."

She stood up and winced a bit. Her right leg looked stiff.

"That was the last time I ever opened those doors. I tried today and I couldn't get them open. I think I lost the key."

"Oh," I said. "Maybe it's in the drawer with the tape."

"No, I looked." Hands on hips, she turned to face the front lawn. "It's just so . . . emblematic. This is hard on you girls, I know that, and I'm sorry I'm putting you through this."

"No, Mom, it's not your fault."

"Yes, it is." She sat back down beside me, wincing a little. "You can't own your victories if you won't admit your failures, you know?"

I kind of shrugged. I didn't know, really. It sounded right, but everything she says does, and it's only later that

I realize I didn't really know what she meant.

"I got an interesting call this afternoon," Mom said.

"Oh?" I hated the tremor in my voice.

"From Kirstyn's mother," she said. "I admit I always kind of thought of her as a little, what? Annoying. A small-minded materialistic busybody, if I'm completely honest."

I sat on my hands to hide their shaking. "Wha . . . Why did she call?"

"She called about your graduation party."

"Again?" I asked. Mom looked surprised at the question so I added, "Daddy said she left a message." I tried to hold down the panic. "What did you tell her? I told Daddy I was handling it myself."

"Yes, well, apparently she called *again* last night after dinner, and spoke to Daddy about your party. He told her he thought that you girls had canceled the party. She said absolutely not, she knew nothing about that."

"I, see, the reason . . ." I stammered, but luckily Mom interrupted me.

"You were working on that angle?"

"Yes."

"I figured," she said. "Well, meanwhile, my check for the down payment for your party bounced. You know what that is, right? When a check bounces?"

"Yes," I said. We were all business, me and Mom, having a quiet little conference there on the front step. "What did Daddy tell her?"

"Kirstyn's mother thought that there was a bank mistake. Your father, I gather, corrected that impression." She sniffed once. Her eyes focused on the hedges bordering our lawn. "He told her that there was an *issue*—that was his word—an *issue* for me at work and we couldn't afford—"

"No! He told her that?" I demanded. I stood up and kicked the step. "I can't believe he did that to me!"

"To you?"

I gripped my jaw tight and stared at the stone landing under my feet. Rain drops were starting to fall. Great, just great.

"When she called me, just before, on my cell, I was blindsided myself."

"What did she say?" My voice was cool and quiet again, like Mom's.

"Well, honestly, she could not have been more gracious." Mom took a deep breath and let it out with a small half chuckle. "She asked how I was holding up." Mom sighed, then continued. "And she said, and I agree, that the adult work world and its *issues* are nothing for you girls to worry about. She said, *Please do not give it one moment's thought.*"

"Meaning what?" I asked.

"Meaning, she wants to pay our share of the graduation party."

"No!" I didn't care that I was screaming. "Absolutely not!"

"My words exactly. I said we were not comfortable taking charity from—"

"Charity?! Oh, my God."

"Right. Her position was that it wasn't charity but friendship."

"You don't even like each other!"

"True. But she meant you and Kirstyn. Apparently you have been a wonderful friend to Kirstyn these past few years. Her mother thinks the world of you, Phoebe. She went on and on about how beautiful your friendship with Kirstyn is and how important it is to celebrate that. She said she actually envied what you and Kirstyn share, because she never had that, herself—close friends she could really count on. She's so happy Kirstyn has that, with you."

She knew. It suddenly hit me. Kirstyn knew. She stood there and took it from me this morning, I realized, even though she knew the truth. *Because* she knew it. "The party is off." I closed my eyes. "I canceled it."

"You don't have to do that. We'll find a way. . . . This isn't your problem."

"Too late," I said. "I canceled it this morning."

"Oh." Mom blinked twice. "Because of my . . . issues?"

"Because of a lot of things."

Mom nodded. "Okay, then. Generous of her to offer, though. I'll have to send her a note. Let's go inside. I have a conference call at three thirty."

She picked up my bag. I followed her down the walk toward the door we actually use, but didn't go up the step. She turned around after she opened the screen door and said, "Come on in, it's raining."

I shook my head. I knew where I had to go.

"What are you doing?" she asked impatiently. "I have to—"

"You said, remember with the tea kettle, the drippy one? You said we are the Avery women; we will never be intimidated." The rain running down my face fell into my mouth when I opened it to talk. I didn't really care. "But I was. I was intimidated. I wanted you to be proud of me. I tried to act strong, be like you, but I'm not. I'm always intimidated. Did you know that about me?"

"Phoebe, come inside and we'll . . . Where do you think you're going?"

I had turned away and was walking the rest of the way down the path, arms crossed over my chest, toward the driveway. "To Kirstyn's," I said.

"It's pouring!" Her BlackBerry was ringing. She wasn't answering it.

I stopped and turned to face my mother. "I thought I was a Valkyrie."

She tilted her head at me.

"But I wasn't. Kirstyn was."

23

By the time the car pulled up the long driveway, the rain had eased into a drizzle. I was sitting on the steps leading up to their walk, soaked through. It was sooner than I'd expected, but track must've been canceled. Kirstyn's mother got out of the car first.

"Phoebe!" she shrieked. "What's wrong? What are you doing here in the rain? What happened, honey?"

I didn't stand up. I was hugging my legs for warmth and my shirt was see-through. "I wanted to talk with Kirstyn."

"Come in, come in!"

"No thank you," I said.

Kirstyn's mother's face switched from concerned to surprised to serious. "Kirstyn," she said. "Phoebe wants . . ."

Kirstyn got out of the car and glanced at me briefly before slamming the door shut behind her and walking toward us.

"Phoebe needs to talk with you," her mother said. "Then come inside and dry off. Okay? I'll cut up some strawberries. Would you like some fresh iced tea?"

"Mom," Kirstyn said warningly.

Her mother slipped into the house without another word.

"You knew," I said.

Kirstyn didn't react at all.

"How?"

She slid her eyes over to mine.

"Your mother told you."

"No." She smoothed her hair back toward her ponytail.

"But you know, you knew, what was . . . about my mom, and everything."

"You're not the only family with an old baby monitor, you know."

I dropped my face into my hands and rocked for a minute.

"I thought we were best friends," Kirstyn said. "When you promised this party would be the greatest thing, all that—you know I didn't give a flying crap about the party, at least not at first. But then I started feeling like, well, you're the one who said it: The point is us. Remember? You said that. The point is us. I believed you. I thought what you were really promising was that this whole stupid party, the flowers, the hideous balloons, all of it—was a celebration of us, of our friendship, and how great it's been, how lucky we are."

"It was. That's exactly what it was supposed to be."

"Apparently not," she said. "Turns out our friendship isn't about being there for each other. It's about you, looking down from Phoebe World to console poor Kirstyn, with her crazy parents and no sisters. When it hits the fan for *you*, though, instead of trusting me, turning to me like I have come to you, how many times? A million? Over and over I tell you my parents this or my life that. But did you come over crying and saying, *Holy crap, my life is going down the toilet, my mother the perfect goddess screwed up and I'm scared?* No, not Phoebe. You couldn't handle letting me comfort you. No way. Admit maybe you and your perfect family had some problems of your own? No, you had a better idea: Why don't I humiliate my best friend in front of the entire school instead?"

I was shivering, hugging myself in my see-through shirt. "That's not what I meant to do."

"Sure it is," she said.

"I wasn't even allowed to tell! My mother is totally freaking out. And I have to, you know, support her. She's the one it's happening to, not me."

"It's happening to you, too."

"Not according to her," I said.

"Well, then she's wrong. It's not just her issue. It's happening to you, too, whatever this is, and you're entitled to tell your best friend."

"Maybe," I said.

"I would've given you the stupid green dress, you know." She sat down next to me, not too close, but on the wet step.

"I know," I said, feeling worse.

"I bet it looked great on you."

"It did," I admitted.

"It looks like crap on me." She wrapped her arms around her knees, too, and asked in almost a whisper, "Am I really such a conceited bitch?"

I shrugged. "Am I really such a distrustful jerk?"

"Yeah," she said. We glanced at each other, then away.

"Hard to believe my mother thinks we're so great, huh?" she asked. "Sounds like we belong in the 'slightly imperfect' discount bin."

"Slightly?" I asked.

We both kind of tried to chuckle, not all that successfully.

"I really meant it," I whispered. "When I promised the party would be great, I really thought it would be. I could picture the whole thing, the best night of our lives so far."

"I know," she said. "Bet you pictured the last dance, too, with Luke."

I started to object, but stopped myself. "Why do you hate him?"

"I don't," she said. "I never said I did. I just asked if you liked him, because it sure seems like you do, and you kept denying it."

I wasn't sure that was really true. It seemed to me like she had made her opinion of him pretty clear. But I wasn't in a great position to argue. "Yeah," I said. "I guess."

"I can't believe you didn't tell me what was going on with your mom." She stood up and turned her back to me. "I would've been there for you, you know, if you'd let me."

"You were there for me anyway."

"Yeah," she said, opening her door. "Of course I was." She let the door slam behind her.

My whole family wanted to know what had happened, but I said please leave me alone and after pushing food around on my plate for a while asked to be excused. I went to bed early, dreading that everybody would act all allergic to me in school the next day. But it was way weirder than that. Everybody acted extremely normal. As if nothing had happened. As if I actually had imagined the whole fight, the whole breakup of our group of friends, everything. Ann was absent. Why didn't I think of that? Lots of girls were watching us, even more intently than usual, whispering, asking one another behind their hands what was going on with us. Was the biggest graduation party in the history of our grade on, or off? Hadn't I screamed that it was canceled? Hadn't I completely humiliated Kirstyn, and myself, yelling like a lunatic outside the school entrance so everybody could hear? And yet, there we were, four out of the five of us, walking down the hall together, heading toward our lunch table. All I could think was, should I go find some other table?

That thought nearly made me cry so I just kind of drifted into the lunchroom telling myself, *Don't think, don't think,* and accidentally sat down at my usual spot. Nobody yelled, *What do you think you're doing, get out of here* (they never would; we never yelled other than that one time when I did), so I opened my lunch and ate it and they ate theirs and there it was. No Sharpies out, no notebooks, the four of us smiling politely but not talking.

On our way out of the cafeteria, Luke caught up to me and asked, "You okay?"

When a person is just barely holding herself together, that is a horrible question to inflict on her.

Luckily, right then Ms. Alvarez dashed toward me and, apologizing, asked if I'd mind using the rest of lunch period to practice my speech for her and the principal, Ms. Clumph. I said, "Not at all," and completely meant it.

I stood on the stage of the auditorium, surrounded by stacks of folded metal chairs and some toppled music stands, reading my words off slightly crumpled pages:

> *Welcome, faculty, parents, family, friends, and fellow graduates!*
>
> *Today we celebrate an important milestone in our lives, and before we move forward, let's take a moment to look back.*

Like ingredients of a good pot of soup, we students started out as individuals. Some of us were carrots, some onions, some barley, and others turnips. But with the dual challenges of time and fire, and some expert stirring by our teachers (Ms. Alvarez cheered at that), *we have changed. Just as oil and heat conspire to sweeten the bite of the onion, and beans soften as they thicken the stock, we have changed, too. We entered Goldenbrook young, scared, and alone. But over these three years, we came together and changed one another. We leave today, still ourselves but now something more, something better. We leave Goldenbrook united.*

United? Ugh. I was barely paying attention to what I was saying; I couldn't or I'd lose it. I was just making the sounds the letters represented, saying the words I'd written down: Our eyes are set on distant horizons, the solid foundation we spring from, or some such garbage. I don't even know. I hadn't ever actually practiced it before; I'd just written it in a hurry after I ate too much of Gosia's White Bean Provençal soup and had other things on my mind.

But they liked it. Ms. Clumph had tears in her eyes when I finished and told me I wrote even better than my sister Quinn did, which is really saying something. I thanked her. Ms. Alvarez told me it was perfect except maybe I could think of something other than turnip because turnip is a silly-sounding vegetable and she wouldn't want people to interrupt my metaphor with laughter. I thanked her, too, but what I was actually grateful for was the fact that the bell ending the period had just rung.

I made it through the afternoon by concentrating on breathing. I didn't talk to anyone, and rushed past Luke when he tried to catch up with me again. *Almost home, almost home,* I told myself the whole bus ride home, and ran from the corner all the way up the street, up the driveway, thinking, *Thank God it's Wednesday,* and that I hadn't signed up for chess club after all. I couldn't wait to be home alone. I closed the door behind me, locking out the humidity and tension.

And then I noticed something cluttering the clean kitchen counter. I think I knew what it was instantly, before it pulled me magnetically into the kitchen to open it.

The invitation.

There, in the purple ink Kirstyn and I chose at the shop next to the salon, was my own name in calligraphy on the envelope (Kirstyn's mom made their housekeeper take a class in it last year), my name and address, my invitation to my own party that I thought I wasn't throwing anymore.

How were our names still going round and round, chasing one another eternally around a neon bright cheery invitation for a party that wasn't going to happen?

It was the prettiest invitation ever. We had designed it ourselves, chosen the colors and the font and the wording. We really loved it.

We.

I never realized how often I think of myself as part of we rather than just I. I? How can that even be a word? I? It looks like a stick, poking up all weak and lonely, alone there with no other letter for company. Which is how I'd felt all day. The air around me had felt so . . . so there, separating me from everybody else.

I was distracted by the air. Well, clearly I had really lost not just all my friends but all my marbles, too. I kept bumping up against the air between us. What a freak!

When my cell rang inside my clutch, I dropped the invitation on the counter. My hands were shaking as I fumbled with the clutch's zipper. Who was calling me? Ann asking what had happened at school? Gabrielle acting like everything was fine? Zhara calling to explain? Kirstyn? Oh, please be Kirstyn.

I got to the phone and saw a name I wasn't expecting.

"Luke?"

"Hi, it's Luke," Luke said.

"I know," I said. "Caller ID."

"Right," he said. "Um."

I picked up the invitation again. So pretty. So perfect.

"I, um . . ." Luke said. "How's it going?"

"All good," I mumbled. "You?"

"Well I got the invitation to your party and I was wondering if, like, if you want to kind of, I don't know if this is what you, were, if, you want to go together? You know?"

"What?"

"I don't mean, like, my mom could give you a ride, which she totally could, if you, you know, need one, but like, I mean you're probably going early with all them, your friends."

"Luke, you were right there. The party isn't, I don't think we . . ."

"Asking you out," he was saying, meanwhile.

"What?"

"I'm trying to . . . Can I start over?"

I had to sit down. "Okay, but the thing is—"

"Phoebe I am practically having a heart attack and it would help me if you just let me get through this!"

"Sorry," I said. "It's just, the thing is, the party is canceled, Luke. Is the thing."

"I'm holding a fancy invitation to nothing, then?"

"Yeah, that's exactly what you're holding, Luke."

"Okay," he said.

"Anyway," I said.

"Yeah," he said. "So, well, see you in school tomorrow, I guess."

"All right," I said.

We hung up before I could get us back to the part where he was asking me out. I sat waiting on the back stairs for my sisters to come home, staring at the invitation in my hands. When they finally came, I followed them up, to tell them what had happened on the phone with Luke, and earlier at school, show them the invitation, and get some advice.

Allison stopped short in the upstairs den and said, "You are acting like a stupid girl, Phoebe. Get over yourself."

"Wh—what?"

"There are bigger problems than a boy you like who keeps asking you out."

"I know," I said. "That's just the beginning. Today was the worst—"

"Pull your head out of your butt. Everybody has stuff going on."

"Did something happen to you?" I followed her to her room and it was only when I sat down on her bed that I figured out what seemed weird—it wasn't made. Allison's bed. I'd never seen it all discombobulated before. "What happened, Al?"

"You don't even want to know," she said, twirling her hair. She looked rumpled, from her T-shirt to her puffy face.

"Yes, I do," I told her. "Tell me."

"Just get out!" She shoved me off the bed, then dragged me out of her room. "You are so annoying!"

"Fine!" I yelled to her closed door. "You lost your chance! I'm a totally sympathetic listener, you know, you big moody nasty jerk!" She didn't even yell back that she didn't need my sympathy. Nothing.

I came down for dinner when Gosia called through the

intercom. All five of us politely avoided eye contact, our forks clanking against our plates loud as thunder in the silence of the dining room. The whole meal lasted maybe fifteen minutes before we flew up the stairs to our own rooms, doors quietly shut.

Thursday morning at school everybody was buzzing about the party again, asking one another, "Were you invited?" "Yeah, were you?" and then jumping around, so excited. I noticed even a few of the brainy girls had brought in *ElleGirl* and *Teen Vogue*, with pages folded down, to consult. All through lunch I tried to get my act together and say, *Hey, guys, what's the deal?* But I just sat there instead, unable to open my yogurt or even my soda, smiling vaguely at everybody, or nobody.

After school, though, I finally couldn't take it anymore. I sprinted down the track and caught up with Gabrielle. I figured it would be easier to talk with her about it than Kirstyn. Other than how fast my legs had to be pumping.

"So what's up with the party?" I asked, trying not to show how out of breath I already was.

She shrugged. Does the girl ever break a sweat? How could a person not be the slightest bit blotchy at that speed?

"I mean, it seems like it's still, like, happening," I managed.

"The invitations had already gone out, obviously."

I kind of grunted. I didn't mean to but I was concentrating on not doing a reprise of my face-planting trick.

Gabrielle slowed down a little. "Listen, I think I know what really happened."

Kirstyn told her? "You do?"

"Yeah," Gabrielle said. "You were angry about the weekend. You had every right to feel left out and pissed off. You took it out on Kirstyn but really you were mad at me. Right?"

"Um . . ." I said.

"I don't blame you," Gabrielle continued. "I should've made a better case to my mom about inviting all four of you. I was a jerk. I'm sorry."

"Oh, please," I said. "It's okay."

Kirstyn had caught up with us by then.

"And in your anger at me, you struck out at Kirstyn, right?"

Kirstyn looked perplexed. I shrugged at her.

"So?" Gabrielle smiled. "Say you're sorry!"

"I'm sorry," I said to Kirstyn.

"Good!" Gabrielle said. "So everything's fine with the party then?"

"Sure. Um, if we run any slower, Coach P will have to time us with a calendar," Kirstyn said, speeding up.

"Oh, yeah?" Gabrielle taunted, racing after her.

I let them go. Coach P yelled at me; I didn't care. I ran alone, and only caught up with Kirstyn at the mirrors after we'd changed. "You didn't tell her?"

She shook her head.

"She thinks the party is still on," I whispered. "Everybody does."

Kirstyn flipped her head down, gathering up her hair into a high pony. "It was too late to cancel. As far as anybody needs to know, you and I had a fight, we made up, nothing's changed. The rest is nobody else's business."

"But Kirstyn," I whispered, bending down pretending to tie my sneaker. "I, my family didn't pay our share. We can't. You know that. I can't."

"So what?" she whispered. I followed her to our lockers helplessly, and fake-smiled good-bye to everybody. Kirstyn took forever gathering her stuff so I rummaged through my bag, too, waiting for her. Finally she closed her locker. I closed mine, too. The last ones there, we headed for the locker room door.

"It's not like any of us paid out of our own bank accounts," Kirstyn mumbled as we walked through the deserted corridors together, toward the main entrance of the school.

"Yeah," I said, "but . . ."

"It's just money, our parents' money. If your parents don't have it to pay right now, that sucks for them, but why should you suffer? My parents will write a slightly bigger check. Nobody else will ever know."

I shook my head. "We'd know. My parents, me. You."

"I'm not trying to lord it over you or anything, Phoebe."

"I know, I'm not—"

"Our parents' money has nothing to do with us. You know you'd say the same thing if the situation were flipped. Right?"

I shrugged. She was right. It's just a lot easier to say money is irrelevant if you are the one being generous. We passed the main office and a gaggle of seventh-grade girls waving tentatively at us. "It's just hard," I whispered. "For me, for us . . ."

"Well, suck it up. Sometimes you have to be on the receiving end, you know?" She pushed open the front door. "So that's settled, then."

I grabbed her elbow and turned her to face me. "I just don't—please understand. I appreciate your, your generosity, and your parents', too. But I can't accept it. I just . . . I can't. And I think it would really hurt my mom, anyway, if I did."

Kirstyn shrugged. "We already signed the contract. The money has to get paid. The only question is who's paying, and that's not really a question either, is it?"

"I guess not," I admitted. I felt completely hollowed out. "I guess there's nothing I can do at all."

"You could say thank you."

"That's not what I mean."

Kirstyn pushed her hair back toward her ponytail and sighed. "Listen, Phoebe. Some things you can fix, the rest you're stuck with. I have a fat ass. You have this family financial disaster. Okay? Not our fault but still our crap to cope with. The only thing for you to figure out is how you're going to act—like nothing happened or like a droopy sad loser."

Her mother was waiting in her big SUV in the center of the circle. She lowered the passenger-side window and gave me a huge smile. "Hi, girls! Come on, get in!"

Kirstyn opened the passenger door; the back door slid open. I shook my head and said, "I'm walking home today."

"Are you sure, honey?" Kirstyn's mom asked. "Are you allowed? I'd feel better if—"

"No," I said, and straightened up. "Thank you anyway! I'm great. It's such a beautiful day. I'd like to walk." I forced a charming smile onto my face. "Bye!"

I waved and walked away, long strides taking me down the hill from school, arms swinging by my sides as if nothing bad had ever happened. I decided on my way home that, no matter what, I had to keep up that act from then on. It's all good. Nothing happened.

I was going for Kirstyn's Option A, and why not?

My friends had forgiven me. Nobody had to know the secrets of my family. Everything had been solved for me. Everything could actually seem perfect again.

I tipped my head up to the sun but behind my sunglasses my eyes were clouded by tears because I knew that even if I managed to fool everybody else, I'd know the truth: Inside, I was in fact the droopy sad loser Kirstyn had warned me not to become.

25

I STOOD ON THE PODIUM, sweating despite the overzealous-
ness of the air-conditioning in the auditorium.

"Welcome, faculty, parents, family, friends, and fellow
graduates!" I started. The microphone squealed. I backed
up my mouth and continued.

"Today we celebrate . . ." I tried to concentrate on what
I was reading, and not on my fingers shaking on the clean
white paper in front of me. Hard to believe I was really
standing up there at the podium, all my classmates arrayed
behind me on folding chairs on the bleachers. Graduation.
Commencement.

"Like ingredients of a good pot of soup . . ." I could
hear every squeak of chair on wood platform, every clearing of a throat.

". . . others turnips."

Oops, I brought the wrong page. I had changed turnips to
celery in the last draft. People giggled behind me. Some

boy said to someone else, "You were definitely a turnip."

I squinted at the page. The black letters danced around. Celery. It said celery, right there in front of me, in Times New Roman 14-point so it would be easy to read.

After a deep breath, I went on. ". . . stirring by our teachers . . ." Nod at the teachers, as planned. Scattered applause. "Just as oil and heat conspire to sweeten the bite of the onion and beans soften as they thicken the stock we've changed too." I was picking up speed. I couldn't help it. *Just get through it and you can move the heck on,* I told myself.

"We entered Goldenbrook young, scared, and alone. But over these three years, we came together and changed one another. We leave today, still ourselves but now something more, something better. We leave Goldenbrook untied."

I stopped.

Did I just say *untied*?

No, I must've said *united.* I looked down at the paper, trembling in my hands. *Untied.* Typo! Spell-check missed it. I glanced up. Big mistake. An ocean of confused parents and teachers undulated in front of me.

"Did I just say untied?"

I didn't mean to say that out loud; it just popped out. Ms. Alvarez nodded. A few kids behind me started giggling again.

"I meant united," I explained, feeling beads of sweat

chase one another from my armpit to my waist. "Sorry. We don't leave untied!"

Now everybody was laughing, even me a little. In a kind of manic, unhinged way.

"That would be weird!" I went on, light-headed. "We leave Goldenbrook *united*. Whew!"

I looked back at my papers but they were blurry now, and I realized I had made the mistake of listening to myself for that one second. I swallowed hard. "We leave here united," I tried again.

No. I couldn't do it. The fake smile sank off my face as I let go of my three carefully typed pages of clichés. They drifted softly down to rest, exhausted and limp, two on the podium and one beside my left foot.

"Okay, we actually leave more untied than united, if you want to know the truth. At least I do," I said, listening to myself with equal amounts of shock and interest.

"What I was saying, about, like, coming here separate ingredients? That wasn't actually true, for me. I came to this school pretty tight with my group of friends, pretty confident, happy. Lucky. I felt like the luckiest girl in the world."

I caught sight of my parents, sitting in the third row on the right. They were watching me with such focused intensity I almost didn't notice they were holding hands.

"I thought nothing bad could ever happen, I thought everything was all good. I thought I already knew the most important stuff—not just, like, how to read and add and all that, but how to be a good friend. My friends always knew I had their back for them. So I thought I had the whole friendship thing down. I was wrong."

I closed my eyes and took a deep breath. *Too late to stop now.*

"I let my friends down. Some of you I let down by ignoring you. And I am sorry for that. Some of you I have been rude to, not confident enough to do the right thing or keep commitments. But worst of all, I let down the best friend anyone could have—by not trusting you, not coming to you, not knowing you'd be there for me. I guess it was just easier for me to keep playing that role of *it's all good*, even when it wasn't."

I sniffed a bit and went on.

"The truth is, I guess, now that I think about it—the reason I thought I was so lucky was because I was pretty, popular, rich. I thought I was lucky because bad stuff didn't happen to me. So then when some bad stuff happened, I started thinking: Now I am unlucky, because . . ."

I looked at my sisters, staring grim-faced up at me from their seats. Allison shook her head slightly. She didn't have to worry. I wasn't doing this to humiliate anybody—except maybe myself.

"I thought I was unlucky because, well, see, there was this dress. A beautiful green dress, and I loved that green dress, I loved myself in that green dress. I could picture myself in that dress, so clearly, dancing in that dress, spinning around in the center of everything, I admit it—twirling around in my perfect dress at our perfect party, surrounded by perfect friends who loved me perfectly on the best night of my already perfect life. And then, for the first time ever, I didn't get what I wanted.

"So I thought, well, now I am unlucky, I am nothing, now that I can't have that green dress."

My mom was looking down, at her hands in her lap. *Damn.* Maybe I was being an even bigger jerk than ever, doing this. *Never be intimidated,* I told myself, wondering what that meant in this situation.

"But I was wrong, Mom," I said, my quiet voice still caught by the microphone, still booming out for everyone to hear. "I didn't need the dress. It was enough to see how you looked at me when I tried it on. I'll have that forever. You saw me, and you liked what you saw. No dress in the world could match that; that's what I've always wanted.

"My father said, when we were fishing recently, that lucky isn't catching the biggest fish; lucky is just being on the boat. I totally didn't get it then but I think maybe now I do. Because here I am. With all of you. I'm not perfect, I know. My nose is running and my mascara is probably a disaster. I messed up my speech and am in the process of making a total ass of myself. Also, I just said the word 'ass' in front of all our parents and teachers. Twice, actually, now. But still, it's all good. Really. Because I'm standing here surrounded by such amazing people. Especially these people."

I lifted my hand to show I meant the whole eighth grade. I wanted to turn around but I didn't think I could manage it, couldn't look at them, couldn't face them. I kept looking at their parents instead, looking now right in their eyes, moving my focus from face to face among my friends' parents.

"People think fourteen-year-olds are awful, and maybe we are. We're moody and nasty and maybe we sometimes have way too much . . . you know, personality. Maybe we drive you crazy, but trust me, it doesn't even come close to how crazy we drive one another. Or ourselves. But we don't completely suck."

I looked right in Kirstyn's dad's eyes, and then her mom's. "Sometimes people can surprise you with how amazingly generous they can be."

Kirstyn's mom nodded.

I turned around, then, and scanned the rows of students, and stopped at Kirstyn. "You are my hero, Kirstyn, the kind of friend I want to learn to be. Thank you." She blinked her big blue eyes twice and I turned away, so I wouldn't completely lose it.

"My friends," I tried to say, but it was hard. I swiped my eyes and my hands came away smudged in black. So much for not losing it.

"What I have learned in this place, I learned mostly

from you," I went on, looking at each of them, each of my friends from Gabrielle to Ann and Zhara over to Bridget Burgess and then to William and finally to Luke. "And maybe the most important thing is—it doesn't have to be 'all good' for me to appreciate how good my life is."

I sniffed hard and stood up as straight as Mom.

"I'm not coming to the party tonight," I said. "Because I don't need the perfect party or the perfect dress to feel lucky. Standing here with you right now, my friends, I just realized: I'm already the luckiest girl in the world."

Nobody said anything, nobody moved. There wasn't a single chair scrape or cough or murmur. "Thank you," I said. "Thank you so much."

Kirstyn stood up. She placed her commencement program on her seat and straightened her gown, then started clapping. A few people joined in, then more and more. Behind me, the parents and teachers were clapping, too. Chairs squeaked as people stood up. My knees were feeling a little weak, but before I could do anything embarrassing like faint, I felt arms around me. Kirstyn's, and Ann's, and Zhara's, and Gabrielle's. And then Luke's, too, and everybody's. We were one huge knot up there on the stage, hugging one another.

26

Floating on a raft in the pool, staring up at the grayish-white sky, I let my wet hair cool my steaming head and tried not to think about it. I had been over it so many times in my mind in the few hours since graduation, trying to gauge what each person said, whether Mom was angry, if Daddy actually felt proud or if he was just saying that, whether Kirstyn had forgiven me or not and what either possibility would mean for next year. After we all finally received our diplomas and got off the stage, but before the whole picture-taking extravaganza on the front lawn of school, Quinn had wiped off all the smudges of makeup from my face while Allison held my hair out of the way. On the way home, in the way backseat of Dad's minivan, they both assured me that I hadn't humiliated myself, or them or Mom and Daddy, too badly.

That's when I decided maybe I could use a swim.

My heart was pounding from all the laps I'd just done.

A full mile. I was determined not to think about what all my friends were doing right then to prepare for the party tonight. Maybe they were still getting their nails done, or their hair. No, probably they were already gathered at Kirstyn's or Gabrielle's, trying on their dresses, twirling around for one another. They'd want to get to the party early, as the hosts, and it had to be past four in the afternoon. Almost time.

I flipped off the mat, back into the pool. Maybe another few laps would be a good idea, I decided, and started stroking toward the deep end. I was reaching for the edge when something hit me, like a bullet, in the back.

Blinking my eyes and floundering in the water, I looked around. Allison was on the back lawn, her right arm cocked, a tennis ball matching the one bobbing beside me clutched in her hand.

"What the hell?"

"I said, come in!" she yelled.

"Leave me alone!" I yelled back. "I'm swimming!"

"Fine," she said, dropping the ball and turning back to the house. When she reached the back door, she turned around and yelled, "But when you finish training for the Olympics, you might want to come in and see what was just delivered for you."

I was out of the pool before she got through the back door, and up the walk before the screen fully closed. "What came for me?"

"Where's your towel?" Quinn asked, coming from the kitchen with a half-eaten peach in her hand.

"I don't . . . it's on the . . . by the pool. Where's Allison?"

She pointed up the back stairs. I took them two at a time, hugging myself in the cold. Quinn followed me up, biting into her peach. We found Allison in my room. A huge garment bag was laid out on it.

"What is it?" I asked. Quinn popped the peach pit into her mouth and threw me a towel from my bathroom. As I wrapped myself in it, Allison grabbed an envelope off the garment bag. "Read the card."

I tore open the envelope. "Congratulations, Graduate!" the front said. When I read the inside, I dropped my towel. I handed the card to Allison and covered my face with my hands.

Allison read it to Quinn:

To Phoebe,

> *It wouldn't be a party without you.*
> *Come.*
> *Happy Graduation.*

> > *Love,*
> > *Kirstyn*

P.S. Thanks for what you said about me.
P.P.S. Wear Quinn's metallic strappy sandals, not your white with the stacked heel—they're so middle school!

I opened my eyes when Quinn laughed. "She never changes," Quinn whispered.

"Thank goodness," I said. Shivering, I walked the three steps to my bed and held up the hanger.

"She had her housekeeper walk it over," Allison said, unzipping the garment bag. Quinn folded the shoulders of it back, over the hanger, and there it was.

My dress. My green dress. Her green dress.

"It's beautiful," Allison said.

"Yeah," I breathed. "It is."

"And you should see Phoebe in it," Mom said. We all looked over to the doorway, where she was standing, perfect as ever in her dark jeans and crisp white T-shirt. "Speaking of beautiful," Mom added.

"Kirstyn sent it over," I said.

"I know," Mom said. "Well, you better hurry up and shower if you're going to do anything with your hair before the party."

"But Mom," I said. "I can't . . ."

"Yes, you can," Mom said. She crossed my room toward me and picked up my towel, and she wrapped it around me. She rubbed my arms through it like she used to when I was little and had stayed in the bath too long. "It won't be easy, but you will walk into that party in that stunning dress with your head held high, knowing that you are loved. You're a good friend, Phoebe. And, what's more, you are an Avery woman."

"A Valkyrie," Quinn whispered.

"A Valkyrie," Mom echoed.

I looked up at Mom, over my shoulder. She kept rubbing; I wished she'd continue forever. She smacked my bottom lightly. "You'd better get a move on."

My sisters helped with my hair, blowing it out, using the straightener, then the curling iron, but ultimately settled on pulling it back into a smooth pony.

Quinn got me her sandals. "Gotta hand it to Kirstyn," she remarked as I tried them on. "They look great with that dress. How did she remember my shoes?"

"No idea," I said.

"*Shh,*" Allison said, working on my lip gloss. "Don't make me smudge this."

"Pretty lucky to have America's Next Top Model doing your makeup," Quinn told me.

"What?" I asked, pushing Allison's hand away. "What does that mean?"

"She's exaggerating," Allison said, back at work on my lips.

"Not too much," Quinn said.

"Tell me," I begged. "Come on, guys. I'm in high school with you now. What happened?"

"Nothing," Allison said. "I just got a callback."

"From the modeling thing you went to with Roxie?" I shrieked.

"Shut up!" Allison's eyes blazed at me, then crinkled. "Yeah. *Shh.*"

"They don't know yet?"

She shook her head. "I don't even know if I want to do it. Anyway it'll probably come to nothing and they'll never need to know. Don't say anything!"

"I won't," I promised. "But, congratulations."

Allison shrugged, but she couldn't help smiling a tiny bit. "Crazy, huh? Ugly duckling like me?"

"Maybe that's the look they're going for," Quinn teased her. Allison turned on her with the lip gloss held out like a sword. While they play-fought, I turned and stared at myself in the mirror.

"Okay, Cinderella," my father said from the doorway. "Your chariot awaits."

Mom drove me over to the club in her Porsche. "Thanks for the ride," I said, partway there.

"Well, gotta enjoy it while we've got it, right?"

"You're not getting rid of this car, are you?"

"'Fraid so," she said.

"But you love this car!" I objected.

"Eh," she said. "Metal and glass. Just stuff. Fun while it lasts. Open the glove compartment."

I did. Inside was a small box with a big bow on it.

"Happy graduation," Mom whispered.

I tore off the bow in one yank. When I opened the box, I turned and faced Mom. "No," I said.

It was her sapphire, the one she always wore. Her thin silver chain, her favorite necklace.

"Kirstyn may be your hero," Mom said. "But you are mine."

The traffic light turned yellow in front of us, and Mom slowed down to stop at it. She lifted the necklace out of the box and circled my head with her arms, placing the chain around my neck. She fastened the clasp and then kissed my cheek, her lips cool against my skin.

We were at the front entrance to the main building at the club, the valet guy opening my door, before I could speak. "Thank you," I whispered to my mother. "For . . . for everything. I'm sorry if . . ."

"Have fun," she said.

"I will." I took a deep breath and straightened up, lifted my chin and then the front of my dress to walk up the steps into the party.

The music was playing already, loud and festive. I walked toward it. I could see people bopping to the beat on the dance floor, a blur of bright colors and bare arms. I stood there taking it in for a few seconds.

"Hey."

Bridget Burgess had walked in right after me, I guess, and now was standing beside me, watching the room ahead of us. She was wearing a really cool strapless dress, white material with black lace over it, and it covered her like skin from her armpits to her knees. Her hair was slicked back in a tight bun and her eyes were lined thick on top, with dramatic mascara and red lips. She looked fantastic.

"Wow," I said. "Great dress."

"Thanks," she said. "I made it."

"You made it? That's so cool. Seriously. Bridget—you look . . ."

"Yeah," she said, smiling slightly. "You, too." She tipped her head up and walked into the room, where a cool song was just coming on, and merged right into the pulsating crowd. I willed my feet to follow her but they weren't ready to go, and so like a game of jump rope when I was in third grade, I stood outside, watching, knees pumping to the beat but not able to make myself jump in.

"Phoebe?"

I turned. Luke exhaled, beside me. His hair was slightly gelled, pushed back from his forehead, and he was wearing a dark gray suit and a white shirt, unbuttoned at the collar, and black slightly shiny shoes. His full lips weren't smiling. He looked hotter than ever.

"Hi," I managed.

"I didn't know if . . . I was hoping you were going to . . . You look . . ."

And then I kissed him. I didn't plan it; I just leaned toward him and was pressing my lips against his before I could think. His hand reached around my waist and pulled me close. I wrapped my arms around his shoulders and we kept on kissing. It felt so good. When we finally pulled away from each other, blinking, we both smiled. His hand slipped from my waist into my hand.

"Hi," he said.

"Phoebe!" Gabrielle yelled, and I looked out toward the dance floor. She was standing in the center, looking absolutely stunning in a low-cut black halter dress and high heels, dancing with her boyfriend from camp. I waved. Beside her, Kirstyn was dancing with Zhara and Anne. They stopped.

"Do you want to dance?" I asked Luke.

"Yes," he said. "But I think your friends want you first." He pulled me back to kiss me again, soft and quick. "I'm so happy you decided to come."

"Me, too."

I walked out onto the dance floor alone.

"You look great," Kirstyn said.

"Thank you, Kirstyn."

"You're welcome." She put her arm around me. I leaned down against her. It was a little awkward. I tottered a little on my heels. She turned me toward Ann, who was holding up a disposable camera. We both smiled as the flash blinded us.

"Hey, Luke," Kirstyn called to him. "Can you get a picture of the five of us?"

"Absolutely." He crossed the dance floor and took the camera from Ann.

As Gabrielle, Zhara, and Ann wrapped their arms around us, Kirstyn turned to me and showed me her teeth. No poppy seeds.

"You're good," I said, and bared my teeth at her.

"You're good, too," she said.

"Good?" Gabrielle asked. "Please! We're the best!"

We smooshed up all close together and smiled.

TURN THE PAGE FOR A
SNEAK PEEK OF

Gorgeous

1

I SOLD MY CELL PHONE TO THE DEVIL.

In my own defense, it had been a really crappy day.

The sun was in full show-off mode again, flattening our suburban town into a caricature of itself—rich, pretty, manicured. The lawns, the women, the girls my age: all manicured. Even many of the dads were manicured. Buffed, of course. No rough cuticles in our town. No rough anything.

"What a gorgeous day," people kept saying, as if they were revealing a wonder, and as if the gorgeousness settled an unspoken argument about our worth. "Absolutely gorgeous!" they agreed with one another. Mothers couldn't stop themselves from marveling out loud about the low humidity, the cuteness of each other's new sandals (and pedicures), the fact that our pools were all cleaned and opened already, weeks before Memorial Day. *Can you believe it? Oh, I know—I love it!* Knees and shoulders reemerged, fake-tanned to perfection, tulips and roses mingled condescendingly with the so-yesterday daffodils, and only a few of the puffiest, whitest clouds accessorized the sky, punching up its cornflower blue.

I was finding it hard to breathe.

Beyond even the migraine-inducing falsetto chatter about the shocking fact that in these days of holes the size of Texas in the ozone layer, it could be—gasp—warm in the late spring in the New York suburbs, my fascist social studies teacher had started my day off by being a complete hypocrite and giving me a B– on my paper. I completely couldn't give a rat's butt about grades, honestly—it is my older sister Quinn's job to bring home straight A's, not mine—but I had for once actually put in some effort, and the only comment on it at all was that I had not gotten my concept approved.

Which was a lie.

We'd submitted our concepts three weeks earlier. The assignment was to write about someone who had changed the course of world history. My best friend, Jade Demarchelier, was doing Eleanor Roosevelt; Serena Smythson, who was apparently not allowed to choose to study Jade, who would obviously have been her first choice, was therefore also doing Eleanor Roosevelt. Leonardo da Vinci, Beethoven, Gandhi, and Shakespeare were other popular choices. I'd chosen to study Gouverneur Morris, a one-legged drunken carouser with multiple

2

mad and murderous mistresses, who wrote practically the whole damn U.S. Constitution including the famous "We the People" section, despite the fact that he thought only *some* people (meaning rich people) could be trusted to self-govern. My thesis was that this "genius exotic" won power for the people in spite of his aristocratic worldview. I still had my thesis statement paper, with the Fascist's two-word comment, the only one on that paper, in her tight-script purple ink: *Interesting! Approved.*

So when I got back my paper on Gouverneur Morris with not one correction on it but only the words *Unacceptable Thesis! B–* scrawled across the top of it, I was beyond pissed. I marched up to the Fascist and said, "Excuse me, this thesis WAS approved."

She tried to argue, but I shoved the thesis statement paper under her beady eyes. She relented, but then started arguing that there were "other problems, too."

She wouldn't say what, though I have a feeling she was referring to the section about his housekeeper/mistress who was accused of murdering her illegitimate child. But the Fascist said, "End of discussion," an expression I seem to be allergic to because it sends me into fits of rage, and that is why I ended up tearing my report on Gouverneur Morris into tiny bits and hurling them at her face.

It is unclear who was the most shocked person in the classroom as the flakes of my report fluttered down over the Fascist's head. The Fascist seemed pretty shocked.

She may actually have been *in* shock, judging from how she froze, other than a slight tremor throughout her body. Or it could have been Jade, who would never ever talk back to a teacher, never mind throw stuff at one, and who stood there staring at me like I'd just sprouted a second head. But I think it might have been me, honestly, especially when the Fascist didn't scream or send me to the principal's office or anything. She just sat there, shaking slightly, allowing the scraps of my report to cling decoratively to her frizzy hair.

It was almost festive.

When the Fascist turned to talk with one of the nicer kids, I walked toward the classroom door. I could see Jade turning to whisper to Serena. I swallowed hard and kept walking, out into the hallway.

"You okay?" a girl named Roxie Green asked me.

"I hate everything," I answered.

"Let's cut second period," she suggested.

"Okay," I said.

She didn't look surprised at all. I myself was by then totally blown sideways. And not just because I'd never cut before.

We walked out the back entrance of the high school and wandered around a bit. We didn't really know each other that well, Roxie Green and I, so we didn't have much to talk about. She had moved out to our lovely suburban patch of hell from New York City over the summer. She lived on my street, down a bit toward the corner, in two houses—one of which, supposedly, was being converted into a rec house: indoor pool, squash court, yoga studio, the works. The rumor was that her family was the richest in our town, which is saying a lot. Some people said Roxie had been a model in the city and the real reason they moved out was that her parents wanted to get her away from the wild life of clubbing and drugs. She looked like a model, that was for sure—tall, thin, and gorgeous. Jade and Serena and I had been eyeing her all year for signs of wildness, critiquing her hair (strawberry blond, very straight, jagged edges), makeup (lots of black eyeliner), and clothes (kind of out-there, weird combinations of pinks and reds, and lots of bracelets).

If she noticed nobody was really talking to her, Roxie didn't show it. She didn't seem to care. She didn't seem to give a crap about anything.

"There is really nowhere to go here, is there?" Roxie murmured.

"Absolutely nowhere," I agreed, checking around and behind us. I wasn't sure if maybe there were security officers, watching for cutters. But even worse, if Jade saw me cutting second with Roxie Green, she'd definitely give me the silent treatment.

"You live down my street, right?" Roxie asked.

"Yeah," I answered. "Welcome to the neighborhood, belatedly."

"Thanks. It sucks."

"You noticed," I said. "You must miss the city."

"You have no idea how much." She pushed her hair back from her forehead with her pinky and thumb. "You know why we moved?"

"No," I said, kind of telling the truth. What I knew was only rumor. "Why?"

"Can you keep a secret?"

"Absolutely," I said. "It's the only good thing about me."

"It's kind of embarrassing," she warned, watching my face. When I didn't flinch, she whispered, "My parents had a sudden urge to garden."

"Ew," I said. "How hideous."

She looked at me with her head cocked, and then nodded. "Beyond hideous. Let's have a pool party."

"Sure," I said. "When?"

"Today," she answered, pulling out her phone. "You know Tyler Moss?"

I'd had a crush on Tyler Moss since September. Once, just before February break, while pretending to look for my sister Quinn in the tenth-grade hall but actually stalking Tyler, I impulsively said hello to him and he hit me with his mitten. I was psyched out of all proportion.

Kind of pathetic, I admit. Jade knew I loved him, but nobody else did. Not even Serena, who would've told the whole school.

"Swim team?" I said, trying to sound blasé. "Dark hair?"

"That's him," Roxie said. "Bring a few friends," she said, and texted at the same time. *Alison Avery and I are having a hard day. Come cheer us up.*

"It's two L's," I told her, feeling like a dork. "A-L-L-I-"

"I thought you needed a nickname," Roxie said. "Alison for short. Do you already have a nickname? Allie or something?"

"No," I said. "Well, my mom called me Allie Cat a couple times when I was little, but I hated that. My dad calls me Lemon."

"Why?"

I shrugged. "Sour personality?" She looked horrified, so I added, "He means it in a loving way, I'm pretty sure."

"Oh." We kept walking. "How about Alison with one L?"

"Yeah," I agreed.

Her phone buzzed. Tyler Moss had texted her back saying only, *Excellent.* Roxie showed it to me and smiled, her dimples deeply indenting her cheeks.

We wandered back toward school as I spilled the whole story of why I'd torn up my paper and thrown it at the Fascist. Apparently it was hilarious in the telling. Roxie's laugh bubbled up and then boiled over, making it seem like I was the funniest, wildest person she'd ever met.

7

Jade stalked up to me in the hall as soon as she saw us round the corner. "You weren't in math," she whispered. "Everything okay?"

"Yeah," I said, and then realized I meant it. "Everything's great."

"Is it?" Jade raised her eyebrows. "I don't want to be late for French." She hurried away with Serena, as always, in her shadow.

"She's a real party," Roxie said, and despite the fact that Jade was my best friend, I felt myself smile a little.

"She's just serious," I explained.

"I don't get it," Roxie said. "You're so fun and she's, like, the tightest girl in the school. Why do you hang with her all the time?"

"Um," I said, thinking, *I'm fun? Seriously?* "I . . . she's . . . we're, like, practically cousins, for one thing."

"You are?"

"Family friends, you know? We always used to rent houses together, Augusts, Fire Island . . ."

"Used to?"

I shrugged. There wasn't a nonobnoxious way to explain that we'd stopped doing that a few years ago, when Mom got her hedge fund job and my family moved to the way nicer section of town and started renting August houses, just us, in Europe.

"Whatever," Roxie said, strolling down the hall as I scurried to keep up.

"We have a lot of history, Jade and I," I said, feeling again like a total dork—but what was I going to do, explain that, although Jade sometimes drove me nuts, nobody else was exactly chasing me around school begging to hang with me, and a person has to eat with *somebody* at lunch? Can you spell loser? So I mumbled, "Plus, she's smart, and . . ."

"Uh-huh," Roxie said, sounding unconvinced.

"She is—and loyal, loving . . ." How weird to be defending the perfect Jade Demarchelier, my own personal Jiminy Cricket, so patient with my cranky selfishness she was practically a saint. "We've been best friends since kindergarten. You get used to her, and then she's great, really."

"She's an acquired taste?" Roxie asked, turning down the corridor toward French.

"Yeah, maybe," I agreed, worn out. "I guess so."

"I don't really acquire tastes," Roxie said. "I still hate grilled eel, and bourbon."

"Yeah, well." I laughed. "I never thought of Jade in quite that company."

"Sometimes a new person sees clearer." Roxie held the door open to the French classroom and whispered, "Seriously. Eel. Bourbon. Trust me."

Madame gave us a slightly dirty look as Roxie and I tumbled to our desks, cracking up while the bell rang. Jade's expression was much more disappointed than Madame's. I had to turn away because that scowl of Jade's

9

actually did make her look a little like an eel who'd sipped too much bourbon, and I was on the verge of peeing in my pants, thinking that.

After French, everybody moved in a blob toward the cafeteria, and for the first time, Roxie sat with me, Jade, and Serena. It was weird. Roxie was the only one who talked at all. I mostly nodded and tried not to smile.

By seventh period, Roxie had convinced me that the *excellent* from Tyler Moss earlier in the day had some possible reference to me. So after school, I had to go dashing home to have a bathing suit crisis as fast as possible.

I let my younger sister, Phoebe, help me choose a bathing suit, because she is beautiful and popular and irritatingly cheerful, so she would know which bathing suit would look good. Also, she is very honest—so if one suit made me look dumpier than another, she would tell me. I yanked an assortment of possibilities out of my closet for her to evaluate.

She chose my new black-and-white print. I pulled on my cutoff shorts, my low-top sneaks without laces, and a loose tank. My hair is impossible, so I didn't even bother doing more than pushing it in front of my weird face, to cover as much of my alien-looking eyes as possible. Over Easter weekend, my grandmother had said I was "interesting-looking." Sweet, right? How clear was it that she meant "ugly"? Especially after she had just been going on and on about how lovely and refined Quinn had become, a classic beauty with such porcelain skin like you never see, and how much Phoebe looked like Mom, so vivacious and getting prettier and prettier every day, before she spotted me and added, "Now Allison, she is more . . . more *interesting-looking.*" Great. Thanks, Grandma. Subtle. I left my chocolate bunny in pieces on her kitchen counter when it was finally time for us to leave.

What a treat, to spend my life between the two pillars of perfection that are my sisters. Joy! Delight! Ain't life grand?

And yet as if I had never met myself, I went la-di-da across and down the street to Roxie Green's, like something lovely might happen with half the boys' swim team gathered at her magnificent pool.

Not having thought to bring his mitten in the 85-degree heat, Tyler Moss completely ignored me, preferring instead to join with his three best friends, one more hard-bodied than the next, in a flirt-fest with the stunning Miss Roxanne Green.

Roxie laughed hard over something one of the boys mumbled. They all laughed along, too.

I almost went in the pool for something to do, until I remembered my hair looks even worse after a dousing. Bored and lonely with only well-muscled backs to look at for entertainment, I was about to doze off until one of the boys accidentally sat on my leg. Emmett O'Leary. My existence had not registered in his consciousness, apparently.

"Sorry," he said.

"Doesn't matter," I said.

Well, that was a lovely interaction.

Then I had a soda. Also nice. Ooh, what a delightful afternoon.

My cell phone buzzed with a text from Jade:

What was up w/ u 2day?

I texted back:

Just another perfect day in paradise.

Meanwhile, Roxie, trying to open up the conversation to include me, said, "Oh, you guys! You have to hear what Allison did to the Fascist today!"

"Who?"

"That's what Allison calls what's-her-name, the social studies teacher with the hair? You know?" Roxie held her hair out to the sides and grinned, her dimples deepening their incursions into her cheeks. The boys laughed appreciatively and never moved their eyes from Roxie's gorgeous face.

"Tell them," Roxie encouraged me.

Unfortunately I started back a little too far in the story, because instead of being impressed with what a badass I was, Emmett O'Leary got kind of stuck on what state was Gouverneur Morris governor of, and it turned into a comedy routine of *Oh, I thought you said he was governor/ No that's his name/What's his name/Gouverneur Morris/And what state did you say . . .*

Tyler cracked up, but it was more *at* than *with*. I knew Roxie was trying to throw me a line and rope me into the conversation. I knew she was not intentionally hogging the attention of the four boys practically panting for a smile from her. It was just a fact of her life.

I stood up and said I had to go. Nobody objected. I walked around Roxie's house down to the street and toward home, answering Jade's next message

where r u?

by texting back

hell.

Phone in hand, I passed three other houses, all well tended, all perfect-looking. *This is where I live,* I was thinking. Right here in hell. Right here, where if you are not gorgeous, you are nobody.

U OK? Jade texted back.

I don't even exist.

??? was all she responded.

Sorry, I typed with my thumbs. *Weird attack. I'm dandy.*

I stuck my phone back in my pocket. It was running out of power anyway, the piece of crap. I trudged home, feeling completely nonexistent, which is a much heavier sensation than it sounds like. *I would give anything,* I muttered to myself (or at least I thought it was just to myself), *to be somebody.*